THE CAMERA AND THE COBRA

Also by Roger Nash

Poetry

Settlement in a School of Whales

Psalms from the Suburbs

Night Flying

In the Kosher Chow Mein Restaurant

Uncivilizing

Once I Was a Wheelbarrow

Something Blue and Flying Upwards:
New and Selected Poems

Editions

Spring Fever

Licking Honey Off a Thorn

Northern Prospects:
An Anthology of Northeastern Ontario Poetry

Philosophy

Ethics, Science, Technology and the Environment:
Reader and Study Guide

The Poetry of Prayer

THE CAMERA AND THE COBRA

AND OTHER STORIES

ROGER NASH

Library and Archives Canada Cataloguing in Publication

Nash, Roger, 1942-
The camera and the cobra : and other stories / Roger Nash.

ISBN 978-1-896350-43-1

I. Title.

PS8577.A73C35 2011 C813'.54 C2011-902136-6

Book design: Laurence Steven
Cover design: Alfred Boyd
Photo of author: Terry Nash

Published by Scrivener Press
465 Loach's Road,
Sudbury, Ontario, Canada, P3E 2R2
info@yourscrivenerpress.com
www.scrivenerpress.com

We acknowledge the financial support of the Canada Council for the Arts, the Ontario Arts Council, and the Government of Canada through the Canada Book Fund for our publishing activities.

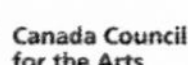

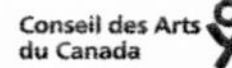

For Chris

Acknowledgements

The author gratefully acknowledges publications in which his short stories have previously appeared: *Bluffs: Northeastern Ontario Stories from the Edge* ("The Choirmaster"), *Cross-Canada Writer's Magazine* ("The Choirmaster"), *Dalhousie Review* ("The Banjo Case," "Sea Changes"), *Grain* ("The Camera and the Cobra"), *Nashwaak Review* ("Growing Up Under a Table"), *PEN/O. Henry Prize Stories 2009* ("The Camera and the Cobra"), *Queen's Quarterly* ("Banking by Mirrors"), *Wascana Review* ("A Conspiracy of Grandmothers", "Houses that Look for Their Keys").

Contents

Abu Sultan

I

The Abu Sultan of my childhood was a small Egyptian fishing village wedged skinnily between the Eastern Sahara Desert on one side, and the Great Bitter Lake—Buheirat Murrat el Kubra—on the other. Since ancient times, it has been populated by fish on the shore side, by sand and cockroaches on the other. Between, a variety of other creatures have achieved a middling existence. In that dry climate, shoots, leaves and flowers put in only a very brief appearance. The village seemed to need us children as somewhat longer-lived human shoots and flowers. It awakened understandings in us that, at the time, we mistook for our own, but which I now realize it had been mulling over forever. If those insights have stayed with some of us, and not been forgotten, if they've withstood the test of time, it's that fishing village which is to be credited with them, not us. We were just lucky enough to be in the right place to have them thought through us. Otherwise, they might have eluded us forever. Sometimes, places do more of our thinking for us than we do.

The thoughts of Abu Sultan came to us children filtered through the omnipresent smell of freshly caught and abundant fish, sometimes even tuna; or, in downdrafts, through the sweetly resinous smell of ripening dates. They came unobtrusively and gently, without shouted dictation, through the small details one's senses are alive to at that age: the click of a goat's hoof on a broken brick half buried in the sand, the distant sound of a bren-gun firing... They started to form at dawn each day, in the voice of the muezzin in the minaret of the small mosque opposite our house. He chanted the Ebed, the call to prayer: "I praise the perfection of God, the forever existing..."

The muezzin's voice rose effortlessly to a higher and higher nasal pitch, like my father's hand-turned Turkish coffee grinder turned fast and eagerly. The eagerness in that voice carried to the shore easily, and even far out across the lake's sea water, as if meant to reach fish fathoms down, too, to bring them to their own kind of worship. My brother and I rushed to the window. We would see four pigeons in the rising sun, floating above the minaret like pages of a newspaper caught in an updraft behind the stern of a stately ship passing through the Suez Canal. Their wings were all in Arabic, and lifted up the light in a dazzle of feathers. That muezzin was blind, as many are. His smoky cataracts looked to us like clouds; not misplaced, but quite naturally relocated in his face. After all, his call to prayer drifted as far as any of us children could track individually recognizable clouds.

II

On rare occasions, the muezzin's voice weaved amongst large raindrops towards us, in its descending register, and hopped, with refreshed devotion, over the few brief puddles to the door. Those puddles, at their fullest, were already nearly drained by the unslaked sand. On such special days, my brother and I dragged old tubs from the cupboards, and positioned them beneath drips and gushers that assembled as rapidly on the ceiling as a boisterous Cairo crowd. The porous mortar the house was built of was short on cement, long on sand; and the flat roof accepted the duty only of keeping out sun, not rain, though we bartered with it frequently. The two of us then engaged in naval battles, in our scratched and dented, sometimes buckled, seas, with flotillas of date branches maneuvering choppily, until breakfast called a truce. It was our firm belief that all battles should defer to meals.

At table, we dutifully organized a trickling umbrella by each chair, and sat as close as possible to the platter of sliced watermelon—from the Nile delta usually, from Cyprus sometimes—waiting for our father to finish shaving. Abu Sultan taught us, early on in our stay there, that something happens to watermelon if you stare at it too hard and longingly. It quickly becomes embarrassingly self-conscious throughout all of its slices. The juice drips down more and more flamboyantly into the dish. The seeds slip shyly sideways into the rich pink flesh. We learned to lower our eyes out of a kind of sympathy.

Mother would run brown water into a kettle, hoping to make somewhat less brown tea. Even after a year, she sometimes still gasped as a small fish leaped from tap into kettle, as happened regularly during a rainstorm. Our water was stored in a steel drum on the roof. A water truck replenished it once a week, rumbling up like a large and rusty armadillo, strengthened to carry its precious load with welded-on circles of plating. The steel drum was not well covered, and water spouts before a rainstorm cradled up small fish, often carrying them to our rooftop, as if to fulfill a standing order.

For us children, it was no gasping matter. If two clouds could relocate in the muezzin's face, and water, rather than news, pour from the radio when father switched it on, fish from a tap seemed perfectly natural. It was just part of the vast orderliness of the world that Abu Sultan was constantly cogitating with us, whereby one thing could switch places with, or turn into, another, in effortless spontaneity.

These cogitations didn't need much reinforcing. They rose up through us, from the sands of Abu Sultan, as eagerly as sap runs up palm trees after a rainstorm. All the same, they were often reinforced at breakfast, on the only occasions when Abu Sultan was almost shoutingly directive. Our mother ate little for breakfast: just one piece of toast with her pot of fish-free tea. She made a little ritual of putting out pots of Moroccan honey or jam in carefully designated places on the table that were, apparently, known only to her. Then, slicing the loaf, she placed the slice in the toaster as solicitously as if she were gently nudging a bandage onto one of our cuts or bruises. Her small and precious ritual was regularly scattered in disarray, unable to befriend the vaster orderliness around us. Moments after she'd nursed the toaster so carefully, there'd be a rustling sound, a flash, and strange-smelling smoke would pour from the toaster, smoke that clearly knew nothing of bakers or bakeries. She'd unplug and open the toaster quickly, giving it a shake. And out would fall what remained of one of the many lizards who kindly shared house with us. Often, the lizard lost only its renewable tail, and scuttled off to grow another. The tail in the toaster would be lightly browned, on mother's favourite setting; but the slice of bread remained obstinately white. For several days afterwards, the loaf stayed untouched in the icebox, carefully maintaining its size; as though, like the lizard, it was trying to re-grow itself.

After breakfast, drips and gushers bounced off our umbrellas with somewhat less of their initial charm. Usually, the rain outside had stopped by then, and even the longest haired goats had been preened and licked dry by the rasping tongue of the sun. Inside, however, the storm continued for quite a while, fed by the lake on our flat roof. At such times, it was more sheltered from the storm to stand outside. This, again, we accepted as no gasping matter. A shelter could become unsheltered, a house become the weather. We'd noticed, too, how, for the desert hawk, the weather became its unassailable fortress-home, which it occupied commandingly. Clearly, there could be strange weathers in people, also, even when the climate outside was gentle and calm. There were days when our father was unsheltered inside himself, but we admired how he stood unbowed in his own pouring rain, until it just as suddenly cleared up.

III

At this time of day, in the holidays, a group of Bedouin boys, sons of the imam and muezzin, brought their game of roving soccer to a crescendo by the mosque. Their aim was to establish prowess and mutual admiration before the rapidly rising sun commanded that only its fierce prowess be recognized until evening. My brother and I joined them, bringing with us, as we stepped from door to game, our own rapidly assembled personal retinue of flies. Twelve such retinues joined us boys in these games, battling for their own kind of buzzing virtuosity. Dark blue ribbons of flies tied themselves to our eyes, noses and lips in tight bows, eager for any suggestion of a bead of moisture, then whirled out behind us as we ran, braiding into thick ropes as we dodged amongst each other. We ended up all tightly knotted together by their sonorous soft velvet, boys and flies, equally humming and alive. It became unclear whether flies were attached to boys, or boys to flies. At such moments, we boys became as airborne as the ball. When we retired to the small café for a drink of iced water, our retinues followed, and hung down in flailing threads from the old flypapers, breaking them off from the wall.

Somewhat tired, but still not prepared to concede sovereignty to the sun, a group of us would gather on the flat roof of a house, and search for any small, mislaid breeze, to capture it mercilessly in our flapping shirts like a frightened quail. You could see the tall dunes of the Sahara, rising in the near distance. They jostled and pushed at each other, marching vigorously towards us. But it was only them shimmering in their own huge ovens. It was then that we would begin our roof jumping. We took it in turns to leap from the rooftop into the soft sand, then climbed up to do it again. The muezzin's brother, the hawk-master, sometimes watched us from below, his lean hawk perched on his gauntlet, nodding its hooded head in approval, the bells on its cap tinkling. Us jumping boys became, in an instant, the uncapped hawks of the hawk-master, turning on each other the wise and hard regard of quickly swivelling slits of eyes. As we leaped into the air, each of us swooped, in his mind, on his most sought after prey. The hawk-master kept a silent tally, smoking cigarette after cigarette with the strain of doing so. Only in Abu Sultan have I seen a tally so seriously kept. As we fell, his cigarette smoke rose constantly, replacing us again and again on the roof.

By now, the sun had achieved uncontested sovereignty. My brother and I would walk back home, for more melon and a siesta. Each of us tried to shelter, as we walked, in the other's shadow. The clear impossibility of this never stopped us trying, enthusiastically. Since when have clear impossibilities dampened one's enthusiasm? We took a short cut on a bridge over the narrow Sweet Water

Canal, that dribbled, in a dry-mouthed sort of way, beside the road. We were careful not to cool our feet in that Canal, which had the uncontested power to turn perfectly reliable feet into an eruption of entirely non-ambulatory boils. Tall alfalfa grew beside the Canal. It rustled and bowed white flowering heads, like bearded elders at quiet and ceaseless prayer in a very sibilant mosque. In the tepid waters of the Canal, spawning frogs floated, spread-eagled and motionless in the heat. They merely drifted to a good place to spawn, their powerful guiding instinct somehow arising out of, and satisfied by, sheer inertia. So it was that, early on in our lives, my brother and I added inertia to the list of possible virtues.

It was here, by the Canal, that we sometimes chanced upon the only other European children in the fishing village, two daughters of an army doctor. They were about our age, but kept almost entirely to themselves, indoors. Abu Sultan could've found few opportunities to think itself through them, but there were some. Their favourite, perhaps only, outdoor occupation, was to catch frogs in a net, anesthetize them with drops from a bottle of ether they'd presumably borrowed from their father, and dissect them on a rock, with a razor blade held in a surgically gloved hand. The older daughter, about my age, did the dissecting. Perhaps she inherited only a curse out of her father's surgical gift. We stayed to watch once only, with horrified curiosity. A hawk or a boy, swooping on a hare that can run for it, was one thing, this seemed decidedly another. They were neat in what they did, perhaps already well trained in needlepoint and sewing. I remember the older girl carefully took out the still attached and beating heart of the frog. The heart dried in a flash in the sun, and a gust of wind coated it with grains of sand, so it looked like a small and expensive delicacy at the bakery. The dying frog, obviously not completely anaesthetized, spread and waved its arms, as if grappling for the first time with human emotions. My brother and I ran off, grappling for the first time with confused and disturbing emotions we presumed were the frog's. The melon slices were carefully avoided when we got home, and we welcomed tumbling into the overpowering sleep of the siesta as if down the shaft of a deep desert well.

IV

We were usually drawn up from the wells of siesta by the arrival of the Bedouin egg lady. She came promptly, just as the day began to consider, as a remote possibility, that it might cool a little. She was almost bald, but that was barely noticeable, as starlings generally circled around her head instead of hair. She came quietly, and never knocked at the door. She tapped at it with her eyes in a very concentrated stare, moving her neck backwards and forwards, as though her eyes were pecking. It was a stare you could definitely hear, and we always knew when she was there. Then she began to barter with our mother, in a voice so startlingly soft, it was as effective as an undeniable command. Every egg in the basket instantly became absolutely necessary for household supplies. That voice was as soft as cobwebs, and one granted everything it asked, for fear of breaking its delicate threads.

The egg lady once arrived at our door in tears. She had just stumbled and broken an egg. Her tears were as precious to her as those small brown eggs. They welled up, but her eyes clung to them, and they didn't fall. They hung from her eyes as though tears themselves were desperately thin-shelled and delicate. Thereafter, she walked so carefully in her rounds, placing each bare, wrinkled foot into the featureless sand as if into an exact footprint she had to match perfectly. It gave my brother and I the eerie certainty that much more than unbroken eggs depended on her never stumbling again. The next stumble could seize up the gears of any passing army truck; or perhaps our father would read in the newspaper that the pyramids themselves had cracked, and scrambled up the whole of history.

It was time for the two of us to put on swimming gear, and head for the waters of the Great Bitter Lake, just beyond the mosque. We followed the egg lady, as she walked the sands as fastidiously as a trapeze artist high above the ground on a swaying, greasy rope. We tried to walk carefully in her disappearing footprints, too, so as not to disturb the day. At this part of the afternoon, men gathered at tables outside the café. They sipped small glasses of sweetened tea, and broke walnuts in a metal dish with a little hammer shaped like an ankh. There was usually a camel tethered nearby, heavily-laden with sacks of peanuts. It waited, disgruntled, for its scorned owner to finish his tea. The more heavily laden the camel, the more superior it looked, and the more pained in its superiority. Its long yellow teeth continued the sneer already well begun by its thick, curled, upper lip.

The roving game of soccer had resumed, flies now cleverly out-strategising boys. But the game didn't rove with us to the beach. Our friends were unsure that salt water was a proper medium for a man, whereas soccer was a princely medium to which even air and earth were entirely subordinate, and in which they could all become sheiks. As we reached the beach, we'd often be joined by our ginger cat, Zoser. He'd appear suddenly, manifesting himself out of the bare trunk of a date palm, if not out of absolutely nowhere at all, as if someone had rubbed his lamp or ears, and he were a purring djinn. He'd trot beside us until we reached the small row-boat. Then, knowing exactly what was afoot, and delighted to be in charge, he jumped into the boat and waited for us to launch it.

Zoser was our cat in a sense of "our" as elusive as the screeching bats he battled with on our roof some nights, clawing them from the sky with scraps of fresh cloud still attached; as elusive as the distant palaces and hanging gardens he got to the rest of the time. He adopted us when we first arrived in the village, allowing us, very generously, to use the rest of the house below his favourite rooftop. He'd disappear for weeks on end, defending his extended harem. He'd return for medical care from the field hospital we became, spreading ointment on the long and courageous gashes of his sabre wounds. Like most Egyptian cats, he was even more proud than he was skinny, and well aware of his ancient past as worshiped by the pharaohs. We named him after the pharaoh Zoser, who's step-pyramid we'd seen in Cairo.

With Zoser arched as tautly as a fur-covered crossbow in the prow, grating his teeth with excitement to guide us, we'd choose a spot to throw out the anchor. All three of us would dive in immediately. We delighted in swimming under water, leaving the now unimaginable heat of the sun far behind us, the other side of a blue and shimmering dome. Zoser would hunt small fry energetically, his paws spinning furiously like the spiked wheels of a chariot. This was one pharaoh who might've survived the re-attached waters of the parted Reed Sea. When he'd caught a fish, he'd return to the boat to exact due tribute. He kept a solicitous eye on us while hunting, sometimes swimming up to us, green eyes as wide open as a friendly seashell. Short bursts of very small bubbles came from his mouth, glittering with a cloudy opaqueness among the columns and halls of underwater light. As they spiraled upwards, it was as though he'd released and banished forever the cataracts from all muezzins' eyes.

V

It was in the evenings, after supper, that Abu Sultan did some of our most productive thinking through us. The darkness outside helped. It blurred the very few signatures that people and history had tried to write on the shifting landscape of sand. At night, that landscape came into its own. It was not so much shaped by human desires, as shaping them, through a multitude of influences. We gain our thoughts from wherever we stand.

In the distance, the donkey that turned the waterwheel would bray, as it made a last few circuits, anticipating fodder and rest. It walked miles each day, only to pass, continually, though the selfsame place it began. Its bray sounded like a rusty hacksaw drawn by a man with exceptionally short and stubby arms: impatient, but determined to get through it. Far out in the Great Bitter Lake, sirens and horns would sound on passing freighters and troop ships. Or was it the roars of a Minotaur, still claiming our times as his own? My brother and I imagined the Minotaur dressed in a white linen suit, smoking cheroots and wearing a monocle, sailing on business to London or Jakarta.

Late one evening, on what, unknown to us, was our last day in Abu Sultan, we were all woken up by a hubbub outside. We ran to the window. Across the road, the mosque was on fire. Its slender minaret burst into the holiest and most zealous of flames: a tapered candle taller than a date palm, intent on illuminating as much of the world as it could. Its call to alarmed prayer dazzled the whole village, and drew in everyone. My father rushed off with a bucket, amongst a crowd of pumping arms and legs, to fetch water from the Lake, but it was a foregone conclusion.

When it was all over, apart from the weeping of women, whose tears turned to uncontrollable spouts of steam on the hot broken stones, the imam and muezzin came to our home. They were uncertain whether the fire was an accident. This was a time of wider civil unrest. The imam advised us to leave immediately, in what we stood up in. An army truck was on the way, to take us to the safety of a garrison. We were perfectly safe—as we already well knew—amongst Abu Sultan's Bedouin, but outsiders might be at work, whose thoughts came from some other, distant, place.

My father asked what they would do about the mosque. The imam stroked his beard quickly and decisively, his hand swooping like a hawk. I still remember him saying, "The desert needs us here, for someone to talk to. It is lonely being a desert for so many centuries. We will build another mosque." He then recited the Bismala, the opening words of any chapter of the Qur'an, "Bismi Ilahi al-Rahmani al-Rahmini": "In the Name of the merciful and compassionate God." His eyes shone, and even the cataracts of the muezzin seemed to flicker with a concealed but determined lightening. Zoser had joined us in the house, disturbed by the events outside. As their eyes shone, he suddenly ran for it to a back room. Zoser was utterly fearless, except for fire. So we knew the fire in their eyes must be real.

That was our last glimpse of Zoser. The army truck pulled up soon afterwards. Its sand-clogged brakes screeched like a thirsty elephant. As we sped off, Abu Sultan looked almost featureless, almost indistinguishable from the surrounding desert. Yet it had helped think the roving soccer players into twelve different people, so colourfully distinct in their moves. As for my brother and I, we would now have to have our thinking done through us by some other place.

Blood Can Pay the Price

Sunset

IT WAS NEARLY SUNSET. There were no boats out at sea. The shore, too, was deserted, but for three robed Bedouin women, sitting in the shallows to cool themselves after another day of fierce heat. The sun, as usual, had blood feuds with people, animals and plants. The women turned their backs to the boy, with due propriety, as he walked by. Wet cloth, freed from the dry logic of daytime light, now concealed only what it revealed, revealed only what it concealed, like a confused would-be prophet. Sand clung to their black robes in small circles, as though they were eager to transform into brown-scaled quietly talking fish in the last of the light, and this was a decisive moment for them. One of the fish burst into song. The boy walked past without looking at them.

A radio warbled from a nearby small mud-brick house. The house was roofed with a sheet of corrugated tin. The tin, in turn, was roofed with a visible layer of roasted air, which shimmered into many different corrugations of its own. Perhaps the radio was badly tuned, drifting backwards and forwards between two stations. For different voices collided, then separated, only to pass right though each other, carrying with them an almost vocal smell of supper: a loud shout of frying sardines. Or was the radio more finely tuned than most, to a wavelength where places, even whole worlds, might collide, might overlap? So the boy wondered, with a start.

The boy swam out from the shore. The edge of the sun just touched the sea, like a gigantic circular saw, poised carefully to cut right the way through. He swam further. There was a call from the shore, but he didn't answer it, since he was already dead. This had happened to him often enough before. He swam further, arms moving powerfully. He needed the sea, and it opened before him with close sympathy. He breathed deeply, his nose held well above the small waves and slight spray. His breath was entirely, and carefully, his own. He swam out to become himself once more, to cast adrift the memory of the school bully who, again that day, had pummeled him down, then sat on his chest, pinning him to the sand, face pushed so hard into his own, that the bully's sour breath had filled his nostrils completely. Then his gasping breath, even his thoughts, had no longer been his own.

A large fish, or one of the now transformed women, swam out past him, nudging his feet. He looked toward the sun again. No longer a giant circular saw, it disappeared slowly over the horizon like an ocean-going dhow, just the tip of its red lateen sail still visible. He remembered a story his grandfather had told him. The sun was the ship of Re, that carried the dead to another world, in the west. At sunset, and until that ship had departed completely, two worlds overlapped. He felt the strong current begin, that would carry him out into the bay. This was a pivotal moment, offering him two possibilities. Facing the sunset, his eyes filled with light from the sea's flaming surface. For a moment, they radiated it back, as though he'd grown into a pharaonic demon. But then he turned back to the shore with a decisive gesture, swimming strongly.

By the pier, an old man shouted down to him, "Watch out! Sea-snake beside you! Deadly poisonous!" He saw the movement of what looked like a very agile piece of rope in the water, between him and the shore. It knotted and unknotted itself vigorously. The sun was just about to disappear completely. With seconds to go, he hauled himself up the closest barnacle-encrusted timbers of the pier, ignoring their sea-honed razor sharpness. Looking back, he saw a dead dog drift out on the tide, completely healthy in appearance, with no sign of injury or blood. Presumably the latest conquest of the snake. His own feet were cut quite deeply by the barnacles. He stood in a growing pool of blood. The old man said quietly, trying to reassure him, "Only the living can pump out blood like that. It's the price of being alive. Not like that dog."

So much can depend on a cockerel

The call of the cockerel from her rooftop releases answering calls from neighbouring rooftops; which, in turn, release the voice of the muezzin from his minaret, to take towering flight among the mulberry trees; which, in turn, releases the sun to climb up date palms, crowing more and more raucous light. So much depends on a cockerel. So Yasmeena always feeds him first, and particularly well.

Her hens gather around her, as she scatters handfuls of grain for them. Their beaks stab at the grain quickly and repetitively, in an even rhythm, like needles of sewing machines when seamstresses pedal furiously at their treadles to meet a quota of robes. Like the seamstresses, the beaks are threaded with sheer hunger. Their pecking leaves marks in the dust, as though her yard has caught smallpox or measles. Then Yasmeena searches the yard for eggs, stretching her hand carefully into dry bushes and discarded crates. Some of the eggs are as small as goat droppings. But the older hens lay eggs like small plump plums.

The cockerel, on whom so much depends, carves hieroglyphics in the sand with his strutting spurs. He's a tireless scribe, endlessly rewriting what the wind smooths away. Only the hens can decipher it: an ancient record of the crowing taxation of pleasure extracted from many millennia of them. So many hens have been mounted, that their clipped wings blur together. The cockerel tips his head to one side, at the call of another cock from beyond the mulberry trees, red eyes full of derision. He blinks suddenly, as if clicking back the hammer of a firearm of desire, lightly triggered to take yet another hen, and yet another. His scarlet comb runs with curling crests along the top, like waves in rapidly incoming and outgoing tides. Though so much depends on him, he's caught in his own ceaseless ebb and flow.

When a boy comes round for eggs, Yasmeena notices she's one hen short this morning. Wild dogs and desert foxes, those she's not so worried about. Poisoned fish guts, laid out at the edge of the desert, have kept their numbers down. Sand dunes drift in more often than foxes at the moment, and no poison will keep dunes at bay. It must be a snake. The death of a hen from weakness or disease, that she can accept. It's fate. Sometimes, at sunset, a hen, weakened by a day of hot sun, and a shortage of brown and congealed water in the irrigation ditch, will ebb away unstoppably with the fading light. But snakes aren't tides. You can do something about them. Yasmeena has her own method of killing snakes.

For her, a sure sign a snake is about, is when the hens cackle and scatter, rather than cackle and gather for the rooster or grain. She searches quietly for its hiding place in a stunted clump of reeds or dry bush. Despite hips sore from bearing many children, she moves like a dervish tightrope walker, robe gathered up in her teeth, stepping gently only into her own previous footprints in the sand, or the scratch marks of the cockerel and hens. The boy follows at a safe distance, balancing in her footsteps in amazed imitation.

She tries not to dislodge any new falls of sand. That might alert the snake. And she walks softly so as not to disturb any wells that might be hidden underground. Wells are like the udders of her goats. In bad years, the whole herds' udders swing flat, like burst and unshaven balloons. In other years, when one udder dries up, another, hopefully, fills. The main thing is not to startle snakes or wells by walking loudly on the earth.

Today, she finds the hiding place with no trouble. She grabs the snake by the tail, whirls it around her head dizzyingly, cracking it like a cold-blooded whip. Then she throws it to the ground, and aims a rock just below its head. The snake's back is broken. Immobilized, like a long and hooded hieroglyph carved in the very hardest of stone, it dies quickly and cleanly in the sun, with no spatterings of blood. The boy watches, wide-eyed, balanced on one tightly bandaged leg in her footsteps.

The journey home

It's the end of another day at school. Convoys of gharries, the military trucks, drive off from the central army school, taking European children to their homes in separate camps and settlements. A guard with a sten-gun stands in each gharry. 1950 in Egypt is a time of rising national pride and civil unrest, preceding the Canal Zone crisis. The children are not aware of historical trends, only of the heat, and that the weight of homework in their satchels adds several degrees to the temperature. The gun might be a toy. They're not sure. They've never seen it used. But they've never seen it unloaded.

Heat breaks in engulfing waves through the canvas tops of the trucks. It drums hard and bright knuckles on their hoods. When a truck slows down, heat ricochets back from it at nearby pedestrians, like an oven door suddenly flung open, slamming into fellaheen carrying hoes, fuming along after them, chasing them hurriedly back from the side of the road. When the convoy leaves the town behind, branches of palm trees, heads of corn, leaves of cotton plants, all vibrate without sound in the sun, instead of rustling: like tuning forks pitched to a blaze beyond sustainable human hearing.

Inside the boy's packed truck, they sit quietly. The less fortunate stand, hanging onto overhead webbing. No one bothers to wipe away sweat any more. They try to keep just slightly cooler in the shade of their own thoughts. At corners, as the truck's gears slip and clash, their thoughts clash and slip into each other too, in sympathy. Anticipations become memories, memories become anticipations. The Pyramids wait patiently for their builders to be born. The Sphinx stands up and stalks off.

As they reach the long, straight coastal road, the boy imagines their truck moving down it like a thick daub of oil hissing down a burning sheet of tin. They pass a dhow sailing parallel to them, just offshore, its sail coloured to pink cream soda by the declining sun. To stay as cool as possible, the boy begins to imagine the truck as a great dhow sailing toward nightfall. They continue driving west. The tires wail as if being flayed alive by the bubbling asphalt. Dogs by the roadside lift up their paws, as if walking on nothing but shards of glass.

How long will the drive to his settlement last? Time passes more and more slowly, even as the truck accelerates to its limits.

The boy knows this slowness is as real as the landscape, not just his impression. They are between settlements now, out in the desert, where time turns into tiny particles: minutes into seconds, seconds into the dust of seconds, and the dust into something finer and more numerous still. There is so much of it, like the desert itself: more and more particles to be measured by the hourglass of the journey. The hourglass threatens to span years, even dynasties. The driver switches on his windscreen wipers, in the hope of brushing some of the dust aside. They beat steadily for a while, as if driven by some inviolable law, perhaps by fate itself. But by the same law, dust returns in even greater measure than before.

The dark interior of the gharry isn't really shade. It's the superheated monotony of a flat and featureless road with nothing to entice the eye. The scarce and leafless trees are neither alive nor dead: like the children in the gharry. The gharry travels for some time without coming across a single human being or animal. At last, a herd of camels, mostly bared yellow teeth beneath balding humps. Even their teeth look emaciated. The gharry passes by the bones of a camel that died by the side of the road. Its ribs stick up, gleaming in the sun like a sand-plucked harp. The land brings forth prophets in lieu of shade; and sand-plucked harps instead of prophets.

The boy stands, holding onto the webbing of the canopy. Beside him, also standing, is a girl new to the school. They sway in parallel. She's not dressed in their khaki uniform, but in a green blouse and white skirt. She's so close, in the packed truck, that her breath moves in and out of his nostrils. He can smell the softness of her lips, the taste of her chewing gum. He tentatively swallows her breath, in wonder. His saliva turns to salt in the heat. He can think of nothing to say. But his body feels so light, it hasn't the slightest need for words.

Like everyone else, both shower out sweat at such an amazing rate, they're as much liquids as people. Swaying side by side, in two parallel streams, they flow down to the rivet-dotted floor together, where the sweat dries immediately. A drop of sweat from her smile falls on his cheek. Though he's never had such thoughts before, he imagines them pouring into each other. Though he's not noticed such things before, he sees her breasts are like small ripe apricots, striving to be larger sweet oranges. They continue driving west.

The bully of the bus pushes between them, and begins to make fun of the girl. The boy can't understand what the bully's fun is about. The bully makes more fun, pointing at a small red stain appearing on her dress. The boy is puzzled by the red stain. The girl looks very nervous, but not unwell. He pushes between the bully and his victim—something he's never done before—and tells him to shut the bloody hell up. The bully is so surprised by something that hasn't happened to him before, that he pushes away and picks on someone else.

They drive on west. The girl gets both more nervous but more self-contained. The stain at her crotch continues to spread. The sun begins to set across the water. The boy struggles to comprehend what questions he should ask. But he's already sure that, though it's been a long journey home, they'll both arrive safely at the settlement in a minute or two. They've both paid the price.

Being bitten by a piece of string

Several weeks later, boyhood ended. It was at a nondescript stretch of road outside the town, on the way to school. Endings and beginnings often happen in such places. The girl in the green blouse was swaying at his side in the school truck, then put her arms around him, clutching him tightly. She panted so vigorously through his nostrils, that he could hold his own breath completely. There was an ululating sound in the air all around them, as of angels or gnats. The truck lurched to a stop. Several holes appeared in the canvas canopy of the truck. More bullets ululated by, as if of two minds about what they should do, and mourning their intended victims. The guard fired two bursts from his sten-gun, shoulders wobbling from the recoil like roughly shaken jellies. Even he seemed surprised it was not mere paraphernalia or a toy. Then all was quiet.

Luckily, no one in the truck was hurt. The boy looked out past the guard. A child about his own age, wearing a blue gallabiya or robe, had fallen by the side of the road. He held a long piece of string in one hand, to which a parcel was attached. As he moved his hand up and down, seeming to wave at them, the string coiled and uncoiled itself vigorously. Then he let go of it, and the loose end snaked across his thigh. It looked as though he'd been bitten by a venomous piece of string. But then the boy noticed, with rising hope, the pool of blood by the curb: it was presumably an injury, not a death. However, the guard pushed him further back into the truck, whispering, "He's dead. Or as good as. Pity he got caught in the crossfire." The boy, in shock, twisted the strap of his satchel more and more tightly around his thumb.

The truck moved off, gathering speed. The boy could see, past the guard, the child in the gutter. He was sitting up, slowly. He waved his hand at them, slowly. He looked right at them. He was shouting, "You're dead now! You're really dead! Really!" A wind from the desert caught the canopy of the truck. It flapped and strained like a sail. They were driving east, into the rising sun. The boy now knew this was completely irrelevant: it would neither save nor take any lives.

He looked down at his hand. The thumb was white and numb, bloodless from the tightly wound strap. In a world where armed guards must take you to school, was this close to being as good as dead? The guard's gunsights swept the horizon. They jerked uncontrollably with each lurch of the truck. One horizon slipped, interchangeably, into another. The truck's gears clashed through each other. The Sphinx walked back, smiling inscrutably, as usual.

The Camera and the Cobra

I

His first posting abroad was to Kasfareet, a village in Egypt, at the edge of the Eastern Sahara Desert and on the shores of Buheirat Murrat el Kubra—the Great Bitter Lake. He'd just started work with the aid agency, as a newly qualified doctor, specializing in a giddying, if not somersaulting, variety of tropical diseases. After flying into Cairo at night, he'd straightway taken a series of hops further south, by bus.

During a brief stop in the city of Fayid, he'd visited a small bazaar outside the bus station. He was struggling with the unaccustomed dry heat, which whittled at his skin like a first year medical student somewhat puzzled by a scalpel. This was compounded by his bewilderment at a strange land made doubly strange in being virtually invisible for large parts of the journey. The moonless desert, that presumably stretched back from the road, had been wrapped in astringently scented and mummifying shrouds of darkness ever since his arrival. At best, he could see only a newly qualified doctor staring back at him through the smeared sheen of the window beside him; as though he'd long preceded himself into the desert, and was waiting for himself—for any one—to arrive there.

Luckily, he'd had the foresight to wonder whether there were any last things he might provision himself with, before the bus took him on to remoter parts. He got back onto the bus carrying a small, brown, old fashioned box camera, which had cost only a few piastres. He settled back into his seat, for the rest of the necropolis of night, and fell asleep eventually. The doctor already in the desert reached for the camera firmly, as it began to roll from his lap. It was obvious that a camera was something he'd long been waiting for in the deserts of his life.

II

In his first weeks at the clinic, patients' symptoms anarchically pursued a life of their own, far from the mountain-cool textbook examples he'd studied in Geneva. An obstructed bowel somehow disguised itself as malaria; malaria as a snakebite; and a snakebite, in an awkward location, as over-enthusiastic lovemaking. At times, he felt as if he were present at an overcrowded and overheated masked ball for anatomists, with heavily cloaked symptoms continually exchanging identities with each other, before slipping away down the slow circle dance of the queuing patients.

The brown, vinyl-covered box camera came into its own in these early weeks, in his time off. Taking photographs became a self-prescribed remedy for his confusion and anxiety. With his camera, as in his medical notes, he developed a mania to record, and perfected his techniques. It also became something of an obsession to perpetuate whatever changed so quickly and unrecognizably around him. He got up early in the relative cool of the mornings, to try and snap the tracks of desert foxes at the edge of the Sahara, even a desert fox itself, before the wind rose and smoothed both tracks and elusive fox back into a shifted and entirely different pattern of dunes. The dunes seemed to lope about as unpredictably as the foxes, and the foxes to ripple about as much as the dunes. They just did so at different paces.

In both the clinic and his time off, he developed a nervous alertness, looking from side to side constantly, gripped by the expectation that something was about to happen that he was in danger of not noticing—until too late. Would the patient's disease turn decisively worse that evening, stalking imperceptibly closer to the kill, like the clinic's cat moving in its strangely motionless sort of way, ears back, towards the chicken roost? Once, through his camera viewfinder, looking for something frameable to snap, he noticed a shy cobra before it slid away. Luckily, a colleague was with him, and warned him to back off, since cobras can spit venom some distance. He got the photo though, very quickly, aware, on at least this occasion, that the camera in front of his face could be as much a blocking and protective shield as an open lens of perception. That photograph took pride of place in his quickly growing album. In it, the cobra reared up like an ancient hieroglyph, spitting its image straight at the viewer across the intervening centuries.

Film was sometimes unobtainable. In those weeks, undeterred, he carried the camera around empty, scoping out the landscape through its viewfinder. He much enjoyed making life frameable, even if it had to remain unrecorded. It satisfied his feeling that, as you can't adequately enjoy anything in the anxious and confusing present, you should at least try to record it, to enjoy more fully afterwards. When his camera was filmless, he usually had a pocket full of freshly harvested and sun-dried peanuts, redolent still with the rich loamy smell of the Nile delta, like an expensive and musky perfume in a forbidden street. He'd crack these open and chew them constantly, while swivelling his viewfinder around, searching for things to remember. He ate the nuts automatically, and was always surprised when he found his pocket empty. Peanuts were certainly among the things he didn't notice enough to enjoy fully in the present. He was more struck by their annoying absence. Absences weren't a memorable part of photography for him, either. A photograph of empty desert, which for his colleagues breathed deeply with its own be-duned spaciousness, was, for him, always a failure: a picture merely of whatever would've been there if he'd snapped in time. Was it supposed to have been a fox or a hawk?—he was never sure. For him, there should always be something in a frame.

III

Near the end of his first month in Kasfareet, when his self-medicating passion for photography was at its height, he was particularly frustrated by lack of film, but framed things in the viewfinder anyway. One dawn, he was walking towards the rising slopes of the Sahara, which already shimmered in a haze from the mere promise of a sun still tilting itself above the horizon like a fast approaching camel train. It suddenly struck him that there was something odd about the camera. It felt heavy for a camera with no film in it; heavy enough to be incorrectly loaded and jammed with several rolls of film.

He knelt down in a narrow valley between two sharp-edged dunes. The valley promptly funneled and tipped light right over his knees, like olive oil spilt from a warmed pan. It almost stung his knees. He opened up the camera. Inside, was a nest of honey-ants. They swarmed to repel the light, clambered over each other's clambering, in a fist-sized ball of rapidly multiplying movements. Their golden, transparent bodies made them look like pieces of animated and highly mindful amber, organizing to protect the distant past from which they'd come, hardening well around their trapped leaves and flies.

He scooped and brushed the ants out quickly, watching them trail optimistically towards a shrinking crumb of shade, and burrow under grains of sand. The bulbous ends of their glassy abdomens, where they stored a sticky nectar, were slightly filmy, and made him think of grainy and undeveloped negatives. How many times, in the last few days, had the clicking shutter of his filmless camera framed and recorded his life among their precious stores of sweetness? As they moved off in a long wavering line, they unreeled jerkily from his camera like scurrying sepia snapshots.

It was an odd thought for him that, just when he'd consolingly supposed himself most in charge at his viewfinder, shaping things, he'd been more observed by the gathering ants, than observing. The thought sent a shiver down his spine that was matched by shivers that flickered down the long, sharp-edged spines of neighbouring dunes. A strange wind was blowing up, one that made him unaccountably nervous. He hurried back to the clinic. Palm trees around the buildings tossed their heads in the wind, clicking loudly, as though tut-tutting in a way that was neither clear approval nor disapproval, but like an old man's absent-minded tut-tutting that was just a resigned acceptance of itself.

As he went in to do rounds, he saw several falcons riding the breeze. They seemed to be gliding to shelter rather than hunting. At a distance, out on the Great Bitter Lake, several feluccas headed for shore at a fair clip, instead of fishing. Their lateen sails strained at such steep angles, even Euclid would've been proud of them. Their wakes tore up deep grazes behind them. There were no clouds of herring gulls in accompaniment. He was mildly surprised, but thought no more of it. He put the camera in a drawer in his room, carefully closed and locked the drawer, then went to open up the clinic.

A grateful Bedouin patient greeted him first, with the gift of a bucket of crabs. He thanked Hassan, and stood for a moment, before starting the day's work, watching the wet and glistening crabs crawl over each other like heavily armoured and disorientated tanks. It was impossible to tell one crab from another. He thought of the interwoven honey ants, as impossibly tangled as a large ball of very angry string. The sight of the crabs both intrigued and disconcerted him. The crabs were so excitingly and assertively alive, waving bent lances and gun-muzzles at each other. Yet no photograph could possibly sort out one from another. They reminded him of the masquerading symptoms that had worried him. Was this, after all, how life had to be, with events—even lives—overlapping like crabs, and presenting as each other? He put the awkward thought quickly aside, and moved on to his patients.

IV

The next morning, just before dawn, the khamsin, the spring wind, began in earnest. He was woken by an orderly coming to his room to close the shutters tightly, and recommend that he stay inside, even though it was his day off. Made curious, he dressed in a hurry and went outside immediately.

A hot wind was blowing from the southeast. The sky was actually darkening around the sunrise, turning clouds the colour and texture of deeply ridged brown corduroy. Thin and ineffectual raindrops were falling that tasted sour on his tongue, like rancid dates, or the beginnings of someone else's vomit. Then the light went from the sky suddenly, blotted out behind wave after wave of stinging airborne dunes of flying sand that flailed at his face. He went inside quickly.

Opening the shutters a gap, he peered out cautiously. The wind blew down directly from above onto the road outside, so that red columns of sand moved along it in what seemed purposeful columns. They swayed and rotated like the dervishes he'd seen dancing. But where the white-robed dervishes had whirled as gracefully as parasols, or the slowly swirling canopies of drifting jellyfish, the columns on the road moved jerkily, stalks of intent congealed blood. Where the dervishes had danced out an enduring measure of the stars, the columns on the road seemed to whir like the hands of a giant broken clock, its over-wound spring driving them round and round crazily. The buildings in the compound, the clinic, the houses, the mosque, all seemed to spin round the columns. At first, it was like an amusing ride on a carousel. But then it seemed as if the world itself was going down a vast plughole, perhaps being poured back, with the desert and Kasfareet, to become the sandy floor of an ocean. He felt dizzy, and closed the shutters tightly.

Sand began to appear everywhere in his room, as if determined to pass beyond mere figures of speech, and give "everywhere" its full meaning. He felt it inside his shirt, filing away at his skin, and buttoned his shirt more tightly. It was in his tea when he poured from the pot the orderly had brought him. There were more freshly harvested grains of sand, than tea leaves, in the pot. When he picked up his fountain pen to write in his diary, it deposited only a few inarticulate blue scabs, instead of words, on the page, and then dried up. When he read a book to pass the time, he always knew what would happen next: sand slid out as he turned the page. It got in his nose, eyes and throat, of course, drawing them all together in common complaint. His voice rasped with bloodshot conjunctivitis, his nose smelt only in prickling blurs, and his sight very nearly went dumb. Sand gradually infiltrated the lock on his drawer. Though he tried every key he'd got, none of them would slide back the bolts on the desert. Eventually, there was even sand under his foreskin. The Sahara allowed no one, but no one, not to be intimate with it.

V

It was his first meeting with the khamsin, that hot wind from the south or southeast during the months of March to May. It is so sand-laden, it flies in as squadrons of airborne dunes, rather than blows in: the Sahara as an eternally vigilant pharaonic Air Force, winged chariot wheels spinning vigorously in the red clouds. Hassan explained the Arabic phrase to him from which the anglicized word was derived: "rih al-khamsin," or the wind of fifty days. He began Arabic lessons over a soup Hassan had made from the crabs. He was pleasantly surprised that the crabs, which had overlapped so confusingly in the bucket, produced a delicious soup in which savours blended seamlessly with one another. Hassan showed him a "secret ingredient" his Bedouin mother had taught him to use: a jar of yellow cummin, looking for all the world like a jar filled with very fine sand by the khamsin itself. He enjoyed learning Arabic as much as eating the soup. His mouth relished both.

The khamsin lasted very nearly the time appointed to it by his Arabic dictionary, but came and went in intervals, with the free-and-easy spontaneity of a genuine, though forceful, conversation. He seldom had time off though, or left the clinic, as there was an outbreak of dysentery, followed by cases of typhoid and then smallpox, and he was kept very busy. He did manage one quick trip, by jeep, to explore the ancient necropolis of Saqqarra. He had barely stepped from the jeep, slamming its door, when a man on a donkey rose out of a dune, as if sound-activated. "My name is Elias," he said, immediately and emphatically, as though there had been some question about this. He offered to introduce some of the tombs. The visit had been memorable mainly because the khamsin had returned with unusual force, and required him to take shelter within a tomb for several hours.

Below ground, in the cave-like tomb, it was almost as cool as spring time in Geneva. Just a few steps away, above ground, they had walked in an endless, whirling oven, that seemed unalterably set on broil. The tomb was that of an important landowner. Elias pointed out a well-preserved wall painting at the far end, that depicted farming activities on the great man's estate. Servants took longhorned cattle to pasture; gave water to a peaceable bull; and carried geese and other foodstuffs, as well as tools of their various trades, on yokes across their shoulders. The figures were painted in such a lively way, they still vigorously served their master in the afterworld of his endless estate; though they'd been doing it nonstop, now, for several thousand years.

Very little sand blew into the tomb. He sat on a rock near the entrance. Using Elias's flashlight, and then his own, he watched the figures at their work. The sheer intentness of their labour, and his enforced shelter from the storm, drew out a matching concentration in him. He wished he had his camera—now unavailable behind a jammed lock; but the scenes drew themselves together for him anyway. The painting did this in such an exact and detailed way, that he wondered, at moments, whether the workmen peered out at him, as a brief diversion between their never-ending tasks, to try and make out his torch-lit gloom.

He could see what the workmen were doing; and see, too, that they knew well how to do it, as masters of their agricultural trades, even if they were slaves of the landowner. Now and again, a thin column of sand blew a short distance into the entrance, interposing itself between him and the ongoing estate work. Then he became uncertain, for a moment, who was doing what. Was that man herding a yoke, watering a coiled rope, or carrying a horned goose? But then the sand sifted down to the tomb's floor, well back from the painting, and the servants' clear musculature, red-brown from their never-setting sun, proclaimed their sweatingly separate activities again. Even in his torch's fuzzy gloom, their wise hands knew what to do. He began to play with the alternating moments of uncertainty and clarity: how the blowing desert covered only to reveal, but revealed only to cover. The sand under his foreskin prickled, and he sensed himself as an intimate part of this process. He looked down at his hands, clutching the flashlight. In the clinic, they, too, were becoming better able to work through the still recurring moments of confusingly horned geese. He raised one hand in unpremeditated salute to the workers, and then felt self-conscious about what he'd done.

VI

He was back at the clinic two days later, very early in the morning, after driving overnight in the relative cool. Hassan had oiled and cleaned the locks to his door and drawer. The khamsin was not in evidence, and the air lolled about among the palm trees, resting itself. Locals told him the fifty days were almost certainly over for another year. He decided to take a quick walk to the edge of the desert, before turning in. He took out the camera from the drawer, which unlocked easily. It needed film, but he'd bought some on the journey back from Saqqarra. But, once more, the empty camera felt strangely heavy. He wondered whether ants had taken shelter from the winds, and opened the camera cautiously. A mound of sand fell in his lap. The camera seemed to have been nearly full of it.

How could ants, then sand, have squeezed, with such yogic flexibility, where even the physicist's thin beam of light wasn't supposed to? But the camera was an old model, and some of his photos had always come out spoiled. He'd assumed it was the developing process. He wiped the camera out, and found the shutter-mechanism was stuck. This was something Hassan would be able to fix. On a sudden impulse, but one that felt quietly sure of itself, he gave both the camera and his recently purchased box of film to Hassan, as a gift. He'd buy a better camera, but there was no hurry. Hassan, delighted, and in the true spirit of hospitality, gave him his mother's jar of cummin in return. Strangely, it looked even more like a jar of fine sand.

After Hassan had left the room, he started to unscrew the top of the jar, to sniff and make sure it was cummin. Then he stopped himself, in embarrassment. How ungracious of him. He was quite, quite sure. Besides, wouldn't it have been fitting, in a way, if it had been sand? He looked out at the desert. It was trackless after the khamsin, its smooth dunes unvisited as yet by desert fox, hawk and herring-gull. It seemed to beckon, to make a challenging gift to him of his always erasable, disappearing and reappearing footsteps upon it.

Doors

I

Alun Davies had rested well on the plane, as a seasoned traveler for his bank. He upgraded computer systems for their branches worldwide. But, though quite fresh and alert, he barely noticed the huge teak door to the lobby, when arriving at his hotel in Stone Town, Zanzibar. Doors aren't there to be noticed on their own behalf. They're to walk though as briskly as possible, and proceed with business.

Once in the lobby, the scent of the island's spiced tea swirled around him, as undeniable as the rapidly approaching storm front of yet another monsoon. He almost braced himself, to hold his ground, as they handed him the traditional welcoming cup. He was a tea-drinking man himself. Stronger drinks—whether coffee or alcohol—interfered with the unagitated calm he needed for computer work. As an afficionado, he found the spiced tea had a pleasantly relaxing effect. Its aroma of roasted ginger, peppercorns, cloves, cinnamon and nutmeg, was stirred in sugary waves by the overhead fan. The air thickened rapidly.

The tea's aroma braided into itself all the other smells he'd been vaguely aware of: the polished leather upholstery in the lobby, his own uncomfortably trickling sweat, the fragrant frangipani outside, the nose-prickling Nairobi dust still on his suitcase, goat dung by the side of the road, unnameable carrion somewhere unimaginable. It made one perfume out of them all, yet without canceling their differences. It left him very much standing where he was, eight steps from the goat dung; yet somehow transported, as himself part of that single perfume, to a place unified beyond all the ragged day-end particulars, perhaps among the date palms and dark-eyed houris of Paradise.

He was pulled out of this uncharacteristically reflective reverie by the tall Swahili assistant manager's welcome. "I know you from before. Glad to see you again. Welcome back. My name is Mustapha." It was as if a most reliable bit of software, tested successfully in the most trying conditions, had crashed suddenly. He knew, was absolutely certain, he'd never met the man before. He'd never been to Zanzibar before. He had a photographic memory for faces, which had served him impeccably well in his career with the bank. He couldn't be wrong. Yet Mustapha had spoken so definitely, in his booming voice.

Mustapha was tall and straight-backed as a minaret, wearing a yellow turban and red, floor-length caftan. He swung up Alun's baggage as though it were no more than coconut husks, and disposed of it amongst porters and maids in a booming voice that carried the natural authority of a strong offshore breeze. From the maids' affectionate obedience, it was clear that women could fall for him just like baskets of ripe plums. But nowhere had Alun ever seen him before.

"What do you mean, you know me from before? We've never ever met." Mustapha's response baffled Alun. It had nothing of the smooth, expected courtesies and apologies he was used to in the banking business. Yet neither did it seem rudely meant, spoken in a quiet and almost confiding tone. "Good not to have met you so many times, before, then. We must have many shared non-acquaintances". Was Mustapha trying to joke away a mistake he'd made? Was it his way of being dramatically obsequious, in the hope of a bigger tip? But Mustapha's tone didn't seem jokey, and his prominently straight back was not that of an obsequious man. With the feeling that he might be missing something, Alun swivelled on his heels and went to his room to sleep.

II

Alun had the next day off. He decided to walk around the nearer parts of Stone Town. Though he left the hotel directly after breakfast, the strong sun had long been at work. Walls in the many narrow streets were both lime-washed and washed in many different shades of penetrating glare. Beams slanted down like cats' agile tongues. They licked at, and warmly encouraged, every patch of spreading yeasty mould that seemed to leap through the lime-wash. Under the sun's leavening effect, gravity itself seemed to stumble and weaken. Stores, warehouses, government offices, a madrasah with neatly uniformed children lining up to enter it, even the sea, seemed to shift, in a familiar and accepted daily cycle, towards weightlessness. The Indian Ocean behind him became a blue, glittering two-dimensional smudge of light. The small children's feet barely pattered, in the dazzle from their neatly starched white shirts. A storefront did a shimmy and shimmered brightly up to its balcony. A vast ambiguity was ruler in the sky. Alun was uncertain, in the heat, whether he was, as usual, merely flat-footed, or becoming superbly light-limbed; or both of them, at once. He stopped for a drink of pomegranate juice. Its sharp, dark sweetness did nothing to resolve the ambiguity.

Alun walked on down a street so narrow that balconies almost met overhead. He remarked on this to a passing coffee seller, making the rounds on a bicycle, with a conical brass pot and a basin of burning charcoal balanced on his handlebars. The man smiled, happy to relay the gossip of history. "Many times, a boy and a girl see one another from their balconies, each side of the road. Their families are quarreling, perhaps; so there's no way to meet. Then the girl gets pregnant. Both the boy and the girl say they never left their balconies, never crossed—really—any space between. So no one gets punished, or not badly. And a baby is born, with that small crack between their balconies as one of its parents." Gripped, and then amused, Alun enjoyed the tale's equivocation. All the same, he got an acidic reflux of that pomegranate juice, and swallowed quickly. How on earth could Mustapha believe he knew him?

Just past the coffee seller, Alun passed a small gap between two buildings, protected by a low wall. Curious, he peered over. Inside was a very narrow graveyard. Clearly, the barber and the digital camera store each side were intimately comfortable with their past. Several of the grave markers were of intricately carved coral, with arabesques of flowing script from the Qur'an. The scripts flowed on unfailingly, like undulating waves propelling themselves right through mid-ocean, with their perpetual messages disappearing and then reappearing among the branches of untrimmed small bushes. In contrast, he noticed that business at the barber's was at a complete standstill. The proprietor sat crosslegged on the step outside, cleaning his fingernails with the intense abstraction of boredom.

Further down the alley, he emerged into a park beside the ocean: Forodhani Gardens, he was told. It was swarming with vendors of goat meat, grilled octopus and samosas. It was obviously a main meeting point. Children played at dolphins on the waterfront; women sat on the grass in saris that bloomed on them as profusely as the surrounding bougainvillea; men gathered in small groups, lighting up frequent cigarettes and conversations. And there, sitting under a fig tree, was Mustapha, presumably enjoying a few hours off. Alun sat down beside him. Though ridiculous, it still niggled him, so he asked, "What did you mean, you know me from before? You're kidding me, aren't you?"

Mustapha looked back at him quite seriously. "It's not kidding. With some guests, I speak that way. It can help them. But let me answer you with a story." He spat out a chewed grape skin on the grass. Almost immediately, ants began to arrive at his feet, in close order. Some carried the skin away, but others waved feelers and stayed, like an expectant audience. Mustapha crossed the four fingers of each hand carefully over each other, like a Buddha or Muslim sage with his hands in a teaching position. Then he began to rotate his thumbs slowly around each other, like a turbine or the propellor on a boat. A dhow, with lateen sail billowing, moved slowly behind him, edging out against the incoming tide. The ever-circling thumbs seemed to propel both story and dhow forward.

III

"Well," began Mustapha. "In that 'once-upon' time, there was a man called Hamdani. He was poor in money, but, to make up for that, very rich in jealousy. He hoarded it, counting it over in his thoughts like a miser all day, away from his wife and working in the field. His wife, much younger than him, was very beautiful; which, or so I've been told, often happens in such cases. She tended the few goats and chickens around their hut, and prepared supper for him from the little millet seed they had.

"His counting out thoughts of her infidelity enraged and terrified him. But his jealousy also gloated over those gleaming, even burning, thoughts, in the way that jealousy, quite inconsistently, does. Truth to tell, he relied on his jealousy to give him his energy. Still, he was far from being a stupid man, and thought of a solution. He would plant mimosa all around their hut. Mimosa, as you know, is a sensitive plant. Its leaves fold when anything touches them. The mimosa would tell him whether any man had visited his hut while he was away.

"It took about a year, because of drought, for the mimosa to grow and spread properly. But, at last, he was protected. He took to coming home early from his field, and looked the mimosa over from the cover of his well by the forest's edge. After only one week of this, his planning was rewarded. There were clear tracks in the mimosa, leading up to the door of their hut. Plants can't lie. So he picked up his stick in a fury. But then he noticed a cat come out of the hut. It took exactly the same tracks back. It was licking its lips, and had obviously been treated to a splash of milk by his wife, while she milked the she-goat.

"Hamdani went back to his field, to hoe more weeds. He was relieved, but in a still somewhat troubled way. So gloating was his jealousy, he knew he would have to see that cat retrace its steps a few more times, for his mind to become properly calmed. But a cat it surely was, as plants can't lie.

"What Hamdani didn't notice, just as he turned his back, was a tall young man leaping and hurdling across the mimosa to their hut, setting his bare feet carefully into the cat's folded-leaf tracks. And when the young man came to the door afterwards, repeating his athletic passage back across the mimosa, the peaceful smile on his face was far richer than the creamiest cream.

"Hamdani's wife ran away the next day. When he found out

what had been going on, he cursed that mimosa. Then he spent three unproductive days hoeing it all out completely, so angry was he that it had lied to him, even when he had cared for and watered it. The headman tried to reason with him, to save him such fruitless labour: mimosa can't lie, you just misunderstood it. But it was no use. He would rather tear out the mimosa, in a rage that made his eyeballs boil with blood, than follow his wife and try to win her back with the beginnings of kindness.

"So, my friend, that's the story's answer to your question."

Mustapha's's story had ended. The ants were re-grouping around other nearby storytelling picnickers. The dhow was out of sight. But Mustapha's thumbs continued to rotate untiringly, as if to propel Alun's response.

Alun had to think for a moment. Listening to a story is several time zones, and long and unconnecting flights, away from reading computer manuals. "So, Mustapha, I was taking your mimosa-like words in the wrong way, when you said you knew me from before. You weren't just mistaking me for someone else; or fibbing and joking to get a bigger tip. But if those were wrong ways of taking your words, what were you telling me?"

Mustapha's straight and unyielding back showed up unannounced at this point, as he stood up suddenly. "I'm sorry. It's not a story's job to explain itself. But, when you get back to the hotel, try walking through the door more slowly." As if to emphasize this advice, he slowed down his still rotating thumbs until they almost stopped. Then he excused himself, and left for work at the hotel.

IV

Bewildered by Mustapha's advice, Alun stood up slowly. He again felt simultaneously both flat-footed and superbly light-limbed in the tropical heat. The leavening of the sun went on undermining gravity. Buildings on the seafront wavered in a haze. They looked about to dissolve, like blocks of salt crumbling into the sea; or, at best, to float off like impossibly light-as-air balconied balloons. Only the slim white minarets of mosques pegged Stone Town securely into place for the midday prayer.

Well, was he light-limbed and agile, or—the very opposite—flat-footed? Alun's training in the exactness of computer languages was programmed into his very backbone. It protested the apparently irreducible ambiguity, as he continued to stumble along so agilely. He tried grasping at the thought that an "x" in algebra can be given many different values. But how can it take them all at the same time? Besides, those values are at least all numbers. Yet, as he now recalled, he'd been simultaneously aware of such different things as frangipani, carrion, dust and goat dung, in that rich aroma of tea at the hotel. Heck, that was as wide open as saying "x" was 7 and a hat and a fish and the onset of true love. He felt an interested anxiety.

At this point, Alun noticed he was passing by a fruit-and-vegetable store, and felt rather hungry. The storekeeper pointed out a pile of big, dark, green-and-brown oblong fruit, covered with sharp thorns. They were about the size of rugby balls, presumably intended to scratch and tear their way into unstoppable goals. "Durians. We call them 'King of Fruit.' Try one. Its taste is heaven." The storekeeper cut one open, and spooned him out a scoop of the creamy, golden flesh within. As he tasted it, gingerly, he was thwacked hard in the nostrils by an abominable stench. It reeked like a wet gundog that's rolled excitedly in a strange mixture of fox shit, mouldy onions and turpentine. Yet, at the very same moment, the taste in his mouth was of an amazing treacle-like butterscotch, with a fine sherry sauce. The smell combined with the taste, as though fruit could defecate energetically and unapologetically in your mouth;

and the taste united with the smell, so that the air was blessed and resurrected to be vanilla-custardy.

The storekeeper and an expectant crowd laughed at his extremely discomforted pleasure. "It smells bad when you cut it open, but tastes wonderful. We say it's heaven in hell," the man said. Alun wondered whether this might not, after all, be an excellent approach to theology. He remembered, out of nowhere, family stories of his parents' wedding and honeymoon in a bomb-shelter. "Love must go on, even in war," his father had said. In his almost retching delight, it no longer mattered to him that he was both flat-footed and light-limbed, happy and anxious at once. It was no different from eating a durian. Clearly, algebraic "x's" were never meant to roll up their sleeves and deal with that.

V

Alun was soon back outside his hotel, quite content with drifting along rather heavily. Mustapha's words about the hotel's outer door came back to him. So he stopped to look at it. It was heavily carved, with brass bosses down a central post. The doorman, seeing his interest, explained that such much-treasured doors were often acquired first—from India or Oman—and then houses built around them later. Termite-resistant teak doors usually outlasted their buildings, and were traded on to one new building after another, sometimes down several centuries. That was certainly the case with this door, as with well over two hundred other such doors in Zanzibar, he said.

Alun began to work out various carved motifs on the door. There were fish, and wavy lines of dhow-crossed seas; date palms of comfort and plenty; a Qu'ranic proclamation of timeless hope inscribed on the lintel. The brass bosses, so the doorman explained, were adaptations of ancient defenses against the battering of war-elephants. A small inserted door, to the left of the central post, was the "female" door. Either men or women could walk through that inserted door, today, the doorman said. "We all enter the world through a woman."

Alun saw that the old door, that had long preceded this hotel lobby as its destination, was recycling, across termite-free centuries, something of all the other arrivals and entries it had once announced. What it recycled were not the previous destinations themselves, perhaps far distant in Oman or India, but the kind of entry it shaped—who you were as you came in. Alun, like so many before him, would enter with his own stubborn hopes, marked by voyages from afar through the wavy and shifting elements, grateful to have eluded assaults and batterings of one sort or another, emphatically in need of rest and comfort. He bent his head, and walked through the female door deliberately. He welcomed being born back into being both completely himself, yet, at the same time, one with all the other shadowy figures who had entered before him. Again, the aroma of Zanzibar tea swirled around him. In it, he could detect both the smell of frangipani and his own sweat. He was part of a single perfume that was no longer, for him, a daydream, but the way the world is.

Mustapha was already standing there to greet him. He smiled sympathetically. "I know you from very long before. Glad to see you again. Welcome back." He held his thumbs motionless and erect.

Houses that Look for Their Keys

I

Yes, this seat is free, as empty as most church pews at the moment. I can see you're a teacher from the school across the road. Taking a lunch-break from the clouds of chalk-dust? I'm a realtor myself. But you'd be dead wrong if you thought all realtors live narrow lives, ruled by that big, overweight buck. People, especially those who went to college, are in such a hurry today, building lives out of bad generalizations. Most generalizations have wet-rot or termites in them, anyway. You look like a pretty thoughtful man yourself, but there you are, probably making the same mistake. Pull up that chair for a bit, and I'll put you right, at least about this realtor.

I went into selling houses after three years of very successfully failing as a chicken farmer. Chickens let you down slowly, or I'd have started sooner. Most chickens are like that, indecisive until they see the hatchet. I won't say "all" chickens, which would be one of those termite-ridden generalizations. Some chickens aren't at all birdbrained. I had one rooster who was a regular Socrates in a toga of feathers, smarter than me sometimes. More about him later. You may think that's a separate story. You're entitled to your mistaken opinion.

I had a natural talent with houses that I didn't have with chickens. I could tell straightaway, from curbside, that some houses welcome you, beckon you in. Others stay stony-faced and sneer "Keep out!" from their tight-lipped guttering downwards. It's funny how few in my profession have this sixth sense, if six is the right number for it. Maybe it should be seven or umpteen. If you thought so, you wouldn't catch me arguing with you. I only took on trying to sell the beckoning houses. When a house sneers at you from curbside, there's nothing you can do to change its opinion. Most clients—and notice, I'll only say "most"—sense this, which makes it hard, if not impossible, to sell to them. About as difficult as selling chickens to a convention of vegetarians. Sorry if you're a vegetarian yourself. You're welcome to it.

Maybe you can tell, I'm not keen on people with degrees in waffling. My younger brother's the only one in the family who went to university. We always thought he had the most wet behind his ears, puddles and ducks, even. He didn't drain those puddles, and now quacks more than ever. But then he never had the benefit of learning from my rooster.

Anyway, I decided to find out for myself exactly what makes beckoning houses beckon—the specific, non-waffling details. Like people, each house welcomes with its own kind of warm-heartedness. It has to do with a lot of little features that all add up to an overall architecturally happy personality. Things like the right kind of colour contrasts in drapes, wall paint and carpets. Even the right kind of echo for voices in living rooms. Then your intimate conversations don't get sucked away into an alternate universe of speechless acoustic tiles, or amplified back at you like a prison guard with a boil on his backside. Learning about these little details, I'd point them out to prospective buyers, which usually—though not always—clinched the deal. As a result, I've had a rather successful career as a realtor. Which is why I'm sitting here in the daytime. I retired yesterday. Yes, thank you, you can treat me to another lager.

But I haven't got to what I really want to tell you. Recently, about five years ago, I started noticing something new about houses, with that sixth sense I was talking about. Truth to tell, this late development in my extra sense isn't one I'm always comfortable with. That's another reason for retirement. Sometimes, on a very first visit to prospect a house for clients, I'd have the eerie feeling that it knew me already. Even when seeing the house only out of the corner of my eye, as I stepped from the car. That was before I went inside and got familiar with it. None of my colleagues have had similar experiences. They can't understand what I'm talking about.

What the heck do I mean, that the house knew me already? Well, its beckoning me in felt a bit like an utter stranger sincerely greeting me as a long lost friend. That, too, has happened to me once or twice, and not only in diners, I can tell you. You're sure he's a complete stranger. Yet, on the other hand—and life is full of that many other hands, you'd think we were octopuses—he seems to know or guess things about you so uncannily. Like your favourite, but little known, holiday spot. You even begin to wonder whether you've met him already, and have a weird amnesia, which has ripped just him out of your photographically remembered album of the past. Or are there ways of being known by people, and very familiarly, which don't involve your ever having met up with them? I know that sounds crazy, and would go against the very best of generalizations. But as my granddad used to say, that's what generalizations are for: questioning even the most hoity-toity of them, to see if there are exceptions. By the way, he once studied, and very seriously, to become a rabbi. But when he questioned it far enough, he found he didn't fit in. So he became a pillar of the establishment in the fish market, instead.

II

Don't think I've lost the thread of what I'm talking about. It twists a bit, but doesn't snap. And where's it written that threads have always got to be straight? In some book in no one's library? Those houses that knew me already, things would happen in them. Like a vista opening up through an arched doorway into another room, with windows and a view of trees beyond, that stole my heart away. I could just stand there and have this feeling seep into me of somehow coming home. I've never had that feeling in my own apartment. Even though bachelors can get pretty attached to their favourite leather armchairs, looking peaceably at the dirty dishes. Once, a strangely placed bannister offered itself up, right into my hand, as I stumbled on a staircase. It turned out to be in just the right spot to save me a fall. I've got an unusual medical condition, genetic I'm told, with a bit of a wobbly right leg. I stumble in some odd places. But they weren't odd to that bannister.

But back to my grandfather in the fish market. You think I'm drifting? Well, think what you like. They'll teach you that freedom at any muddled college. People even get government research grants for it, I hear. I've got a bit of Jewish in my background, through that grandfather. Not enough to call a fast or even slow cab for the synagogue, as there's a lot of pernickety Irish in me, too. But I do like reading history now and again, about what might have happened to my folks in the past. Of course, it might also not have happened to them, as I don't know exactly who they were. But that doesn't make what might not have happened to them any less interesting. Anyway, something that I'd read began to nose up real close, like a spaniel suggesting a companionable walk, to that feeling of being at home at last in strange houses.

Sometime in those Middling Ages, all the Jewish folk in Spain were driven out of that country. Had to leave everything behind, just to carry their lives with them: houses, sofas, horses, you name it. But one thing many did take with them were the keys to their front doors. They left so fast, they needed, desperately, to carry with them the hope that they'd come back one day, and let themselves in again, perhaps greeted by the same old spaniel in the hall. Those keys got passed down, carried all over the world, as successive generations moved about, sitting on lumpy sofas, or just lumpy ground, in many different countries. I hear there are some of those keys even in Montreal.

Whether granddad had such a key, I didn't know. There was talk of an immigrant ship lost in a storm, sunken cabin baggage, and a corroding key passed down the digestive tracts of generations of fish, as they spread out in their own deep diasporas under the seas. My grandfather certainly found some interesting things in the guts of fish as he cleaned them on his stall. But to tell you about that would be drifting more than the fish. All I have of his is an old pocket watch from Russia, still ticking away patiently, like his canny old heart did under that smelly waistcoat that was so richly embroidered with wet fish scales. Also an ornate, coppery pipe scraper that he used on the plug of burnt baccy in the bowl of his curved meerschaum pipe. That pipe belched enough smoke to cure most of the fish in the market.

I guess the old Spanish keys that survive will fit only breezes in carparks, now. If any of the original houses still stand, who remembers a wandering ancestor's wandering memory of where the heck they are? And doors and locks must've been kicked in and changed a hundred times. Still, if any original locks have lasted, you could try your key for ancient ownership, see if it turns back the rusty bolts of the centuries with a time-travelling screech. More likely, you'll find that a bit of prime real estate, that you'd love to own in a universe governed by old keys, rather than young property lawyers, just doesn't fit your key at all. Then even if that house makes you feel you're coming home at last, with your wobbly right leg known about so perfectly, you can put the house right, even if sadly. Look! The key just doesn't fit, you've got a case of mistaken familiarity, good as it is for my ego. Like convincing someone you've taken an instant shine to, that they can't know you, as you never grew up in Pookahoolie Falls, wherever that is.

All this helped me get clearer about my problem with the old houses in town that seem to know me. I'd no chance of convincing them it was a case of mistaken familiarity. I didn't have original or even old keys to show as misfits for any of them; only shiny keys for newly fitted deadbolt locks and security systems.—Crime has been on the rise in my part of town.—And those keys, entrusted to me by the prospective sellers, all fit, of course, though I certainly don't.

I seemed stuck with an unresolvable fantasy of being known by strange houses: a fantasy I couldn't test and narrow down, lock after misfitting lock. And unfocused fantasies, as granddad Izzy once said, will lose you the most money at horse races. You've got to study the form, and saddle your imaginings to that.

III

Let me pay for this round of drinks. At this fourth drink—and don't they evaporate quickly?—I should introduce myself. Name's George Berman. Who says you've got to introduce yourself at the start of a conversation? Where's the stone that's chiseled in? In someone's fancy rock garden, the very worst selling point of a property? But here's a real clincher to my story. A few weeks ago, scanning the newspaper closely, to avoid that stack of dirty dishes catching the slightest glimpse of me, a couple of items smacked me in the eye. They were on different pages, but seemed very connected to me. People always assume that writing things in a sequence, on different pages, orders your thoughts. My brother Sam, the one who went to university, still tries to convince me of that. If he's entitled to his educated mistakes, I'm entitled to my own opinion. The newspaper's sequence usually seems sheer chaos to me. Publishers should leave newspaper pages unnumbered and only loosely shuffled, and let readers sort out an order for themselves. But don't assume we'd all arrive at the same sequence for any day of the week.

On one page, in the middle, there was a fairly small report on a commercial development in Europe. A big corporation was building supermarkets in Spain. To do this, it was leveling streets of unsanitary old houses. Some were where there had once been a ghetto. Protesters were trying to stop them by lying in the way of the bulldozers. The corporation was outwitting them, as corporations often, but—you've got to allow for exceptions—not always, do. One protester said that the leveling was being done in the strangest of circumstances. The bulldozers came in at night, virtually soundlessly, and left no rubble behind. He said it was almost as if the old houses had shaken themselves awake in the moonlight, after centuries of sleep, got up, and walked off on their own, trailing bits of rose bush and shrubbery. As I scanned the print, I could hear the surprise in his voice. Pardon me, you can laugh into your drink if you really want to, but why shouldn't it make sense, at least sometimes, to say you can see what things sounds like?

Then, on the front page, there was a big story on the previous day's bombings of Iraq. Apparently, some carefully programmed smart bombs were landing very accurately on target, but on-ground investigation later showed there'd been nothing there to hit. The military spokesman wasn't prepared to admit that anything had gone wrong with the bombs. So what options are left? My brother said it must be something was wrong with the maps and aerial photographs that they used to program the bombs. But he frames a lot of decorative "musts" with his degree diploma. And why need he hang it just inside his front door, where it jabs you in the eye? Anyhow, even my rooster, when I was farming, taught me more than Sam's featherless professors taught him. You can get more than two options for answering a question. For the rooster, it wasn't either meet his maker via my hatchet, or keep the hens happy. He just flew off one morning when I left his coop ajar. That taught me a lesson about options. So, a thought suddenly hit me. Maybe the targeted houses just upped on their own, and went off somewhere a lot less disturbing. You drink a lot of laughs, don't you? Why not stick with them, and save on your beer money?

I'll try a whisky this time, but don't think it's drink doing the talking. Houses shift themselves? True, it flies whack in the face of all our generalizations about houses, all the familiar probabilities and impossibilities. But what's wrong with that? People once thought Earth was the bull's eye centre of the universe. Until careful observation showed us it's more likely an insignificant part of some deity's unfenced and tangled backyard. Something he's not even noticed enough to put up for sale to any other subcontracted deities that may be around. Probably something that wouldn't sell if he did, seeing the state it's in. So, on what city planner's computer disk is the clear ruling stored that houses can never be on the move around the world, discreetly and under cover of darkness, especially when they're threatened? It's like the cats of a city in Europe I heard about. They all walked out of town together, hours before a bombing raid began in the Second World War. Now isn't it improbable cats would do that? But the cats probably thought it just impossible that the people would stay. For that matter, isn't the whole sweep of human history just a bit far fetched?

Then I put two and two together. So what if my answer seems five to you? If you're dealing with rabbits, it'll definitely, and soon enough, be more than the over-familiar four. If you only get four, there's something wrong with the sex life of rabbits. Are some houses trying to rejoin keys passed down over hundreds of years, and that's why they're on the move? How do you know that's absolutely impossible? Can't wingless man fly, now? Perhaps houses yearn for the families that owned them, just as people get homesick for their homes. Houses certainly have feelings. Most of my colleagues in the realty business agree on that, even the hardest-nosed. You can be struck by the mood of happiness or sadness in an empty home, sometimes in one particularly room. And the feelings are in the house, not us, just tired, numbed and sweaty from the realtor's workaday routine.

IV

Could you tell them to bring tea, my throat's getting a terrible drought? It seems off on its own on a packaged tour of the Sahara. Now where was I, if you can remember? Ah yes, we're going to talk about holidays, if you follow where I'm going. A few weeks ago, I confirmed the final calculation, putting two and two together and arriving at a definite five. I'd taken a week's vacation down in New Orleans, in that beautiful old French Quarter. A colleague lent me keys for a property he'd had no luck selling there, and told me I could bunk down for a few days. I thought I'd practice my retirement a little, beforehand, in case retiring is like playing the violin.

I arrived in the evening, and stepped off the streetcar, suitcase in hand, into a jungle of tropical jazz. Tangling vines of sound wove out of every small bar I walked by. High notes on the clarinets pushed their tendrils right up walls, to loop in and out of that haciendah-style metalwork of the verandahs above. You could hardly tell where clarinets ended and arabesques of ironwork began. Though I bet dogmatic music teachers would disagree, it could equally well have been the other way around. You couldn't tell where the fluted railings ended and the clarinets took over what the buildings themselves had begun. From the start, I could tell all this was getting to me more than you can let happen in business.

The house I was to stay in was down a side street, hidden in swaying shadows, but I'd no trouble finding it. It beckoned even when the shadows got as black as alligators' tails in a swamp. But then, be darned, I couldn't find the key my friend had given me. I thought it was in my jacket pocket, but then remembered I'd absent-mindedly slipped it into the suitcase. It didn't seem a good idea to unpack the case curbside in the dark. Knowing me, I'd lose a change of socks, maybe even the curb. I was wondering whether to walk back to one of the better-lit bars, when I glanced at the lock on the door.

The lock had an antique look to it. I wondered whether it might be graciously amenable to being picked. The corner of my credit card wouldn't do the trick. So much for banks. Then I thought of trying the coppery pipe-scraping rod of my grandfather's, that I keep on my key ring as a talisman. I poked at the lock in an embarrassed way, hoping it would be too polite and antique to complain. Suddenly, it felt as if the pipe-scraper were being pulled in forcibly, given some irresistible access code. I heard small parts of an intricate mechanism click and slide back. The rod didn't just poke in, it somehow fitted.

I'll snip a long story short, as you're looking at your watch. Believe me, you can't sell a house either, unless the lawn's clipped. Mind you, the story'll only grow back more bushily than before. What's wrong with that? That's the right way for stories. Well, if you follow where my story's going—and it's not meandering, it's just the longer short way, with more scenery to it—I own that house now, and move down next week. As soon as I stepped into the hall, I had the strongest sense of coming home to a place that I fitted as perfectly as any pipe-scraper its lock. The building seemed to know me well, too. My wobbly knee was anticipated uncannily by some oddly placed handrails. And a picture on the wall, of a bearded old guy, had just the dusty, scratched-up eyes of my grandad, though I didn't recognize anything else in the face. That picture went with the house. The eyes smile and ask questions like his, and follow me everywhere.

As for the pipe-scraper, I've figured that out. Might go to a locksmith to confirm my opinion. If he has a different opinion, he'll only get it out of a book. The pipe-scraper didn't just pick the lock, it fitted it as its own key. That key was probably passed down the family line, until people forgot the original house, and even that it was a key. For my granddad, it was just a good pipe-scraper, and probably his father used it that way, too. So, where in the universe is it written that a pipe-scraper can't have been a key? There you go, with termites in your generalizations again.

True, a Hispanic styled little house at that street corner doesn't date back much over a century. But there's something odd about the dusty town planning records. They show an empty lot in 1882. Yet the very next year, they list an "old and established" building at that site. My brother would say, with his college emphasis, that the records must be wrong: that either the building was new, or they got the lot number wrong. But suppose the records are right? Who's to say the house didn't just take itself there, one dark, Jacob-dreaming night, to the town planner's drunken amazement? It's been waiting there ever since, for granddad Izzy or me to come along.

Well, you're not saying it, unfortunately, as I see you're leaving. Still, though I'm only talking to myself now, it's as my old rooster once showed me. Life's about there being more than two options. There's more to life than hatchet or hens.

A Tale of Two Menus

I

Tom sat down at the sidewalk café near his hotel, to order a coffee. It was the start of a week's holiday in Amsterdam. He'd best shake off the numbness of that day's long flight there. He was surprised to be handed two identical menus. At second glance, they were identical but for items on one being twice as expensive. Then he remembered what a well-travelled friend at home had told him: in Amsterdam, any twice-as-expensive menu includes marijuana as an unnamed ingredient. He had no intention of repeating his friend's experience, and misfiling three unremembered days of his life, even missing a flight home. So he took care to order coffee and a slice of apple pie from the cheaper menu.

After the coffee, he walked over the cobblestones to a small metal pissoir by the canal. Standing within the narrow strip of its encircling barricade, he was embarrassed to find how much of him, below his flies and above his waist, seemed on very prominent display. Passengers on a passing barge waved at him cheerfully, and tried to start an animated conversation. He felt deeply confused by this merging of public with private. For a moment, he was disconcertedly sure he was wearing cloudless blue boxer shorts under Amsterdam's shared tartan sky. Coming out again, he noticed the sun was already beginning to set. Shadows were spreading across the cobblestones like oily pools of water. Disoriented for a moment, he had to pick out where the café was. Still thirsty from the dehydrating flight, he went back to his seat, and abstemiously ordered a cheaper-menu glass of mineral water.

He sipped slowly, relaxing into the approach of evening. Departing sunlight gathered around the water in his uplifted glass, and sparkled in it. It seemed to be leaving his glass last of all. The blind girl in the street didn't stop smiling. Her smile glittered off the coins in her out-held cup. He threw two more glitters into the cup. He was definitely flush with light.

Nearby, two dogs drank endlessly at a darkening horse trough. The trough began to mutter itself murmuringly full again, with water or with shadows, from an automatic stop-cock. At the next table, a man who looked like a biker, dressed in leather, held his large, red-haired fist above his head. Though he clenched it tightly, waving to the overworked waiter, light ebbed from it too. Apparently disappointed, the man thumped his table hard, pushed back his chair, and followed the light quickly.

II

Tom paid his bill, and walked, with what he noticed was an odd mixture of questing aimlessness, towards the sound of music. A street singer, in a red flamenco dress, was singing in what he took to be Spanish. He understood the sadness of her song perfectly, though not its words. He stood as close to her as he decently could. The song smelt of cream sherry draped in a black mantilla. She tongued the sharp sadness of her song between teeth that she pushed out like the white tines of a rake. When the song ended, he was surprised to see that the seams of her black net-stockings went on zig-zagging silently to the same rhythm.

The crowd swayed on beyond the singer, and Tom was drawn along with it. At moments, he half wondered whether the crowd wasn't as much caught up in him as he in it; or whether both of them weren't caught up in the same strange, starlit, citywide, entirely diligent lack of direction. He began to notice more and more of whatever was going on around him. He was pleased to find many tall, slim, young women around him, pushing bikes. Their legs soared up inside their jeans in a curved energy that barely ended at the flaxen firework displays of their ponytails and caps. He was fascinated by how the soft click of their bicycle chains matched the gentle rolling sway of their hips, which bobbed up and down as if on small and increasingly excited waves in the Zyder Zee. For a while, he found himself unable not to walk behind one particular girl in the crowd, because her hair turned to gold under each streetlight. The closer he walked up to her, the more golden it got. But she turned round and stared at him. He felt his feet instantly turned to lead, cat-box clay, wet mud. He remembered, then, that young women are the best of all alchemists.

The crowd flowed, with one joint, unfocussed mind, into a large, cobbled square. The food market was over, and stalls were being taken down and packed into unanimously red pickup trucks. The much larger, and more ancient, bird market was beginning. Doves and herring-gulls set up stalls around mounds of discarded ice-creams and french fries. Tom discovered they bargained fiercely and unfairly, but dealt in anything bar orange peel. He traded two gum wrappers for one bent feather, which he stuck in his lapel.

As the crowd left the square, a stiff breeze blew black-headed gulls onto the rooftops. There, as far as he could tell from a distance, they instantly became the crumpled, wet pages of yesterday's newspapers.

Suddenly, Tom realized they must be passing though a street of the red light district he'd heard so much about. Lolling inside their red neon-lit windows, girls blew kisses at him as plentiful as bubbles, pressing lips, cheeks, whatever they could, against the glass, like exotic fish in an aquarium. Behind them, he could make out large, neatly-made beds, rather than the usual scale models of treasure chests and Davy Jones's undersea castles. One of the rooms was deliberately poorly lit, and all he could make out was a pair of luminous, rainbow-striped panties, swaying invitingly back and forth, as though they were gravity free, and had plans of their own. In a moment of clarity, he realized that the panties, entirely on their own, had irrevocably altered the order of the universe. They were wearing someone, hidden in the shadows, not being worn by her. He began to wonder what it would be like to spend the night with a pair of prime, rainbow-colored panties, after you'd peeled off the merely supporting woman, and folded her carefully in the wardrobe.

Mesmerized by what he saw around him, Tom had slowed down. The crowd and its questing aimlessness moved on, and he found himself alone in a dark side street. How would he find his way back to the hotel? He stumbled about for some time, trying to retrace his steps. Churches with brass-studded doors kept on looming past him. Eventually, he realized it was the same church and door, and that the apparently disordered stumbling had been executed in well-bred circles. He decided to go and sit in the church for a while, to catch his breath. As if waiting for him, a bell began to toll from the steeple. It sounded cracked and dull-toned, as though trying to speak of something other than time itself, but unable to remember quite what. Pigeons flew in high pizzicatos of wing-flaps around it.

Sitting in a back pew, he calmed himself by slowly breathing in that always unmistakable vintage church air. As usual, it had been prepared, by an age-old recipe, from the smell of damp, salted herring and a Carolingian treatise on heresy. There were some faint lights at the front of the darkened church. Someone began to play hesitantly at the organ, as if practicing. The tempo picked up, as notes started to remember each other. Then a fugue swept down in such fast, glittering glissandos, that only the notes could have had time to remember each other, whether or not the organist remembered exactly how many fingers he had.

Outside the church again, Tom quickly got his bearings. He now recognized the church tower as one he'd seen from the café near his hotel. After a quick walk, he was back at the café, for a pot of herbal tea before going to bed. He was tired, but had that rare and satisfying feeling of having accomplished much that evening through doing nothing at all.

III

Again, the waiter laid two menus before him, with a large, inviting flourish, like a toreador waving his cape at an uncooperatively stationary and cautious bull. There was a young Dutch couple at the next table, dressed, in carefully planned anachronism, in Beatnik gear. The man smiled at him. "Hey, why don't you try the more expensive menu. It's cool, man. Eat and drink a bit of that stuff, and you'll really see things." Tom was not so inclined, and ordered from the cheaper menu. But, with a sudden surge of curiosity, and not wishing to snub the conversation opener, he asked, politely, "What sorts of things d' you see, then?"

The couple giggled so quietly and easily, they must've been well into a later course of the more expensive menu. The young man reached out and squeezed his partner's thigh lingeringly, as though his hand were sutured to it, and he'd be badly hurt if he tore it away. "Well, man, you know what the real killer is? When we walked by the canal, on the way here, I couldn't stop thinking her hips bobbed up and down like just the prettiest of yachts. But now, I'm really into seeing her hips just as her hips just as her hips. Pure and simple hips, that's what I dig!"

Shading his eyes carefully, Tom gazed, with covert admiration, at the hips in question. Then he glanced down at the two folded menus on his table. From what his new Beatnik friend had said, he could surely be quite certain he'd ordered from the right one. Because, to his eyes, there was nothing simple about such beautiful legs. They looked as though global peace might start from them the very next moment; and, perhaps, already had.

IV

After finishing his herbal tea, Tom went to sit in the church again, just for a moment, to collect his thoughts before getting an early night. Sitting in the back pew, he noticed an old man kneeling by the altar. The organ playing had stopped, and the church clamoured with centuries of silence. The old man bowed his head in prayer. Then, he heaved his chest awkwardly, and clapped an embarrassed hand to his mouth. But he couldn't hold back a long, wheezing belch from the deep despair of his digestion. It rose straight up among the gothic pillars; trilled lengthily through quarter-tones of Bartok and the twelve-tone system of Schoenberg; alternated pianissimos with fortes; modulated into different keys and far-flung centuries; floated past statues of saints in their niches; grew harder-edged among the marble folds of their robes; swelled louder past the displayed instruments of their torture; fanned out amongst the vaulted tracery of the ceiling; eventually became a triumphant and jubilant boom in the domed face of the Pantocrater; fading at last into the distant gold of his halo.

Tom was startled onto the very trembling edge of his seat. He'd never heard anything so movingly and unquestionably not hallucinated. He went to bed straightaway afterwards. As soon as his head touched the pillow, the old man's anguished epiphany of wind soared up in his head. Tomorrow, he could safely eat in that café again.

The Choirmaster

I

Until yesterday, this open field still had its own choirmaster. It looks a perfectly unremarkable field, lying fallow, full of nettles and stray garden flowers. There are three nearby cottages. The next houses you'll come to after these are five miles away, on the other side of the pine forest, outside the town. To tell the truth, there are more garden flowers in the field than in the gardens themselves. For the past ten years, the cottages have had a remarkable run on tenants, and been empty at times. This was never good farming land, and the road into town is bad in winter for reaching the factory on time for your shift.

There is talk of the cottages being pulled down next year. But bets are being laid, the cottages will beat the landlord to it. The shingles and thatching on the roofs have turned a menacing gangrenous green. Some of the windows are warped into squints that would make an optician despair. I went inside one of them last year, visiting a patient, and had to climb down through the front door. The foundations have started straying as adventurously as the garden flowers. Yet, unremarkable as the field and three cottages are, there was once a noisy village here, with its own small tannery. If you brave the nettles with some good high boots, you'll soon see that they grow out of the mounds of fallen walls. You can still make out the floor plan of the tannery, and of the even smaller church.

But it's the choirmaster I wanted to tell you about. He died last night, in his sleep. He'd lived here in town with a nephew for years. He was ninety-six or seven. Though he, his nephew, and the official records were of several minds on that. I've had him as a patient since I first set up practice in Zaminsk, twenty years ago. He must've been in his seventies then. Though he outlived them both, two of his cronies would turn up in the waiting room with him each Friday, as reliably as sneezes after snuff. There they sat, warming themselves at the stove, busily buttoning and unbuttoning their thinning grey waistcoats. There was nothing really wrong with those three, until the days they died. They kept well until everything stopped. But on Fridays, they'd run out of tobacco, and come to see if I could possibly prescribe some of that herbal tobacco I kept in the dispensary then.

Those three took to arriving just before I closed up the office. I'd let them sit for a while by the stove. They'd wrap and re-wrap the small twists of tobacco I slipped to them. Perhaps it was their many years of practice at it, but they could pack a room so full of pipe-smoke, that the next morning even the floorboards would smell like a mixture of freshly cured cod and ham. Sometimes his friends would call him "Choirmaster." "Well, Choirmaster, what do you think of the price of wood?" "Remember, Choirmaster, the night before we left for the Army? Remember that barmaid, Miriam?"

I had no idea what a choirmaster should look like. Should a choirmaster look like anything at all? Still, he didn't look like one to me. His hands were thickened from what was surely a lifetime of hard work, labouring. They seemed no more capable of having stirred a musical instrument than is a ploughman's foot. Though he had a resonant voice, I never heard him sing or hum, to while away the tobacco-waiting time. Nor did he whistle, though his two friends sometimes did, and rather musically too. Still, there was something respectful in their use of the title "Choirmaster" that whittled my curiosity to a sharp point. Whatever made him a choirmaster sounded far more interesting than the determinedly straight hair that had earned me the nickname "Curly" as a boy. So I took to sitting and talking with them for a few minutes, before turfing them out into the snow, still smoking like storm clouds, and closing up shop. The few minutes occasionally became rather longer, even though I had a beautiful young wife and a new baby at home. For you don't often meet a man who took forty years to find out that not everything is music.

II

Where he had got it from, he didn't know. His parents both worked long hours in the tannery. They preferred to drink themselves directly into a drowse of an evening, without any pretentious detours though singing and dancing first. They went to church only when the priest could frighten them into it, which was not very often. And once there, they no more joined in the hymns than the stone font they hid behind. That, too, was also rumoured to be entirely unimpressed by Christianity, the faint carvings on its pedestal being of pre-Christian origin.

It was the priest who first noticed it in him. A carriage from town clattered into the village, horse and driver in a sweat and trembling hurry. It was a banker, looking for the house of the foreman of the tannery. This must've been just before the turn of the century. "Choirmaster" was only four or five at the time, and most eager to help such magnificent horses, and even anyone with them. He'd called up to the driver that the house he wanted was one with a boot scraper outside that sounded just like this. Then he'd kicked at the metal railing by the wall where he was playing. The driver had thrown up his hands in disgust, and urged his horses on in search of someone less demented to ask. Luckily, the priest had been visiting the house with the railing, and overheard the whole incident. Acting on a hunch, he took the boy into the choir, where he shone from the first.

He'd thought nothing of it until the priest took him in tow. But every boot scraper and railing in the village made a musical note for him. He could tell the exact pitch of each. They just sang out loud and clear, especially in the hardest frosts. That was how he knew the different houses, not by the numbers on one or two of the most imposing doors, or by what faded shade of red or blue the drapes were. After talking with colleagues over the years, I've found out just how rare it is to be gifted with this affliction. For him, even noses got blown in different keys. For instance, his father and the shoemaker's apprentice had quite different looking noses, one long and pointed, the other widely spread by a well-placed punch. But they wiped their noses in the same key. He'd noticed it first one evening, playing by the river. The apprentice's girlfriend was sitting on the bank, her man sprawled out beside her, his head laid gently on her lap. There was the comforting familiarity of water singing by, and then the apprentice's sneeze. The man had seen him, and surprised him by scrambling further into the shadows under the tree. But that was not before a last dawdling ray of light had revealed that the apprentice had his father's face.

It was not only unpleasant surprises that his odd skill brought him, though it brought him enough of those. For it could, on occasion, help him get through events that thoroughly rattled those around him. Apparently, his grandmother was a terrible procrastinator. She made no exception of her deathbed, and seemed to draw it out as long as possible. I must admit I've noticed that in my patients too. Decisive people are much less likely to hang on at the end. Anyway, even at his grandmother's deathbed, an invisible *basso profundo*, which he accepted was heard only by himself, had interposed itself on the events, screening them for him through a great rumbling stave. The floorboards vibrated, and a fine powder of soot fell rhythmically down the booming and chanting chimney. The high winds and the voice went on patiently for days, until her eyes rolled up and made a decision for her.

He told me, with only the faintest smile tucked away in the corner of an eye, that it was his ears that helped him through harsh winters where others lost both their ears and lives. Coming inside from the loud silence of the snows, his hands would feel as heavy as frostbitten turnips, slung at the ends of his wrists. They would tingle and pulse painfully back to warmth, in time with the richly interwoven sounds that welcomed him in the house. There was the creaking artillery of the floorboards; the faint but pure sound of water being poured very slowly into a tin pan in the kitchen, like the highest note you can reach on a violin without spilling a drop; and the dog scuffling about as eagerly as a whole pack of excited and badly trained castanets. A younger brother would bow over his hands, and scream with the pain of returning fingers. But he himself could sit down quietly, and take the cat on his lap, stroking it stiffly with those strangely vibrating turnips, coaxing it like a bewhiskered keyboard, kneading into it the rhythms that throbbed around the tips of his fingers. The cat would stop purring, and narrow its eyes into abrupt slits, its ginger fur beginning to bristle.

He quickly became principal choirboy in the church, and the choir doubled in size for the pleasure of singing with him. He made great strides on the organ too. He was playing it once when the bishop was visiting, and the bellows began to give out. Mice gnawed through them at least twice a century. The shoemaker's assistant, the one who had been the apprentice, was doing the pumping at the time. He pumped faster and faster, doubled up, sweat running away with his eyes, like a womanizer in Hell condemned to genuinely please all his abandoned conquests at once. But the music kept dying. Without missing a note, he modulated through key after key, until he reached the right one to quickly pick up the church accordion, and continue without a break.

But it was the choir that was his true love. Once, when I had stayed talking by the stove later than usual, he told me that singing in the choir as a young man was the closest he had ever come to possibly believing in God. There was something about how faces in the choir became warmed by their rapt attention. Apprentices and millers of the most dubious habits were transfigured, on a perfectly regular basis, into beings with the faces of young men or angels in the priest's prints of da Vinci; undecided for the time being about sex and even their own mortality. Sometimes the eyes of one face or another in the choir stalls opposite would shine suddenly, as if looking out from a great nimbus of light that was gathering itself up behind the whole choir. He sang at his best then, for the light had its own purity of sound, and he tried to imitate it; though he was not otherwise able to hear or sing colours. On these occasions, it felt as if his voice was rising straight up out of the top of his head.

The village choir was becoming of some note in the district. He was all set, at the extraordinarily young age of eighteen, to become the new choirmaster, at the bishop's request, too. The old choirmaster had died unexpectedly. Then the Great War broke out. He and most of the choir left for the front. The younger ones swung their legs backwards and forwards over the edges of the cart that took them into town, singing flawlessly in three parts out of a sun-speckled cloud of dust. The axle energetically kept whatever time was appropriate.

III

At the front, his hearing soon impressed the sergeant. He had an uncanny knack for detecting the exact location of enemy gun emplacements. He could tell, too, whether incoming shells were going to bother them, or fly overhead. He would listen intently to an enemy offensive opening up in the pine forests opposite. It made him think of a band of giant bass players, warming up for a particularly vigorous barn dance. Machine-guns fired at a noticeably higher pitch as they heated up in action. He could even tell from this when they were about to jam. His company had a string of remarkable successes in taking machine-gun positions, and with very few losses. He gained a bit of a reputation for himself, standing up in forward trenches, in a clear line of fire, and conducting enemy guns with the butt of his rifle. He used some elaborately obscene gestures too. He would do this for several seconds at a time, until his ears told him to watch out for himself. Even so, he had some near misses. It was this sort of performance that gained him the nickname of "Choirmaster". His company went on to suffer severe losses, but only after he'd been invalided out with a leg broken badly in a fall from a gun carriage. Medical records generously did not report it had been serving as a podium at the time. So it was that he spent most of the war in various garrison towns, in charge of pipes and drums for ceremonial occasions.

At the end of the war, he returned to the village, and was promptly inducted as choirmaster and organist. He had the difficult task of creating a choir from children just out of diapers. For of the choirboys who had gone off to war in a singing cloud of dust, only he and his two cronies returned. These two were lucky enough to be nearly mortally wounded early on in the fighting. They had escaped from the front on stretchers. The old priest's original hunch really started paying off now. The choir gained a reputation for itself, even in the capital. The Choirmaster told me that, after ten years on the job, he felt he'd trained not only a choir, but every rafter in the church too. I can remember pushing another log into the stove then, to prolong the conversation.

In hard winters, when distant lake ice boomed like slowly tolling bells, the rafters grew more and more brittle and active. They rang out interminably in a cascade of abrupt twittering chords. He delighted in improvising on the organ, even during services, to let them all fit in. Perhaps his ears were growing acuter still. For, soon after the death of his parents, he found the stone font responded with a grudging hum to the deepest organ pipe. Eventually, it worked up enough enthusiasm to go on humming gently to itself for a short while. Though only he noticed this.

It was about eighteen years after the war, during one of the coldest winters of the century, that things changed for him. It was right in the middle of a service. The rafters were excelling themselves in accompanying him on the highest notes. His attention was suddenly tugged away by a giant bass voice booming out from the front of the congregation. He could just make out a small man, dressed in a shabby black coat without any buttons. He was alarmingly small for the size of his voice, which almost seemed to own him. He didn't recognize the man. But the voice sounded remarkably like the one that had interposed itself for him over his grandmother's last breaths. He found himself unable to look away from the man, who abruptly turned on him two eyes that were as black as the buttons his coat was missing. Things certainly started happening then.

He lost control of the rafters first, which began to sound like nothing he had heard before, just a hacking overhead, beams coughing in no key at all. The font fell stubbornly silent. Something seemed to be going wrong with the organ. For a moment, he wondered whether mice had been mating with the bellows again; then remembered that the bellows were new. Besides, his assistant was pumping them in his usual dreamy and unhurried manner. For the first time, he heard clicks from the keyboard as just so much interfering din, as were wheezings deep from the interiors of the organ pipes, and a loud and provocative belch, as a faulty connection relieved itself unashamedly. He remembered looking in desperation at the choir stalls opposite, for the least encouraging hint of that great cloud of light that waited behind the eyes of the sopranos. But even the usually bright brass crucifix snuffed out as he watched. It went as dull and grey as slate. The keyboard now made as much sense to him as if it were spinning maliciously backwards and forwards beneath his fingers. The music got knocked over, and he had to run from the church.

IV

He must've asked everyone in the village who that man in the church was. The one with eyes as fiercely unrevealing of whatever he felt as two black buttons; and that big voice towering over him. No one seemed to know. A few old grandfathers coughed reflectively, then spat out their opinion. Even so long after the Great War, an occasional soldier would still wander his way back from across the border. Church records showed that, over the centuries, strange birds of this sort had not infrequently been sighted. It was usually slap-bang in the middle of quiet times, when whatever conflict was last had been forgotten as conveniently as possible. It was because the border stayed close, whichever way it decided to shift. Those wanderers just came and went. Eyes got that dull and blank only in certain circumstances. Such men had probably chosen to keep wandering, after the last frantic engagement. Long roads forgive everything. Exhaustion is the next best thing to regaining your innocence. You're too tired to feel answerable for anything in the end. Believe them, they said, it comes with old age too.

At first, the Choirmaster couldn't help thinking the stranger in church had brought him misfortune. But that idea slowly receded, like a well-lanced boil. Anyway, whatever brought it on, the change in his sense of the musical seemed permanent. Being so suddenly unable to hear everything as music left him too confused at first to hold the simplest tune in his head. It got swamped in the racket around him. But he eventually got used to this. He could pick out, as well as the next man, a barmaid's song from the friendly brawl staged by apprentices for her admiration. But he had lost his appetite for making music. A hymn that was no longer caught up in the counterpoint of chanting rafters, what kind of thing was that? It seemed a small thing, a trivial thing, in tune only with its own short-lived self, and not with the wider and patiently enduring world.

He resigned from the post of organist and choirmaster, and took to farming on a field near the church. The old priest at first wouldn't believe, and then wouldn't accept, the resignation. A large widow from the village was engaged on a temporary basis. She stayed on as temporary organist quite permanently. The Choirmaster's name was still listed in the church records as official incumbent, though no salary was entered beside his name. He was carried into the limbo of "indefinite leave" on the point of an accountant's pen. Some thought the priest acted out of kindness, and in the hope of encouraging the return of the Choirmaster's skills. But perhaps it had as much to do with his hopes of a comfortable retirement. The musical reputation of one's church was known to count with the bishop at times like that. Either way, it made no difference to the Choirmaster. He went on farming, and his ears shied away like a spooked horse from letting him back into the church.

He and his two cronies were called up for the Second World War a couple of years later. He had a hard time of that, all right, and fought right the way through it. No conducting the shells and gunfire this time. They returned to an empty field and three cottages. A lost bomber, who knows from which side, had released its bombs here. The church and the tannery had helped it lighten its load, and the houses had caught fire afterwards. The church records were salvaged. He was still down as choirmaster. The records were placed in the archives, beyond the reach of change and accountants. He was on "indefinite leave" as choirmaster for ever. They'd made their way back to the village as quickly as possible. But he was not surprised to see, in a cracked mirror in one of the cottages, that his eyes had all the makings of a pair of prize black buttons.

He got a job with a builder in town. It was a good job. There was plenty of rubble to turn back into houses again. After he retired, he visited the field and three cottages more and more frequently. He began to have dreams in which his father floated up to him and sneezed in key. But sneezes like that happened only in his dreams. Toward the end, I used to take him out to the field myself on occasion, when visiting patients. You could see him through the broken back windows, shuffling around out there, poking his stick inquisitively into the mounds of nettles. His head often seemed slightly raised, as if he were straining to hear something he just knew must be there. It gave rise to some colourful rumours among the remaining cottagers, I can tell you. Was the Choirmaster coming back to conduct again, in the middle of an empty field? On his last visit, yesterday, he even seemed to be waving his stick about in the air. But, then, we've had a bad summer for flies, as I'm sure you've noticed.

Growing Up Under a Table

I

He grew up, in his early years, under a grandmother's table. Thousands in his generation did. His birth certificate, if accurate, would have given that table as his mother's most recent address: "Oak table from Harrison's, carpenter at Fordingbridge, circa 1889; two flyleafs, nice woodgrain, ink stains in one corner, pot rings in places, needs refinishing, bids to start at 20 pounds sterling." Many other mothers and children had addresses in cupboards under stairs, or under kitchen sinks. It should come as no surprise if psychiatrists discover that many adults, today, have recurring identity crises, in which they worry that they'll never amount to much more in life than damp mops or buckets. Like so much in life: both funny, but no laughing matter.

Things got crowded when other adults came and stayed under the table, as they generally did on the nights of loud noises. It was hard to tell where your foot or hand ended, and someone else's eyes or nose began. He often got into trouble for trying to blink with his foot, or to unclench his nose. Outside the table was something he heard called "the dining room." It wasn't used for anything in particular. There were several very comfortable looking armchairs scattered about, but no one ever sat in them. They seemed there just to hold an endless conference of chairs. Outside that, again, was something called "the house," but it wasn't often visited by him.

Even under a small oak table, somewhat pot stained, you can still grow up, coming slowly into your manly estate. His grandmother sometimes wondered, aloud, whether it would have been better for him not to have been born, as the times were so noisy. In later years, he recalled, or imagined, his grandfather replying that, though that might be true, who amongst them had ever had the luck never to have been born? It was easier to have your horse win in the big race, than to be unconceived. The odds must be fifteen thousand-to-one, against. If someone had had the luck not to have been born, he hadn't met that gentleman, yet. In general, the consensus was that, if you're born already, and here under the table, you should make the best of it, and please get your foot out of my mouth.

It was under that table that he learned to stand upright, take his first steps, and develop that important evolutionary distance between himself and whatever other crawlers live under dining room tables. He enjoyed walking, but knew, by second nature, to turn at end of the table, so as not to come out from beneath its shelter. His mother was insistent about that. He wheeled about even when his mother wasn't there, and he was quite alone. Perhaps it was because he was a fairly obedient child. But it was also because he enjoyed the challenge, as he grew a bit taller, of walking upright when his head scraped against the underside of the table.

Today, when he's grown taller than the underside of his own hair, and no longer resides at any table address, you can see a groove on the top of his balding head. If he wasn't kicked by a mule, I'd say that's the cranial diary of his early walking experience.

On just a few occasions, there'd be the delight of a visit to relatives. Then he'd go, in his mother's arms, to stay with Auntie Dossie, who lived under the stairs. It seemed a long way off, outside "dining room," though still inside "house." There was less scope for walking, as the quarters were cramped. However, he could learn how to jump under the high, steeply sloped ceiling, but mostly on the spot. It was a needed addition to his ever-widening interests. The main attraction at his aunt's, though, was the box of wooden building blocks she pulled out from a corner at the back. They'd been stored there since her own childhood, when, apparently, people lived quite differently and strangely, walking anywhere they pleased, all over the house. Why they'd want to do that was beyond him. It seemed a pretty silly thing to do, with so much noise about. He was glad, as children always are, to have been born into a more enlightened age. He got good at building towers with those blocks, that were even taller than himself. This particularly pleased his aunt. His towers rarely tumbled down on their own. You had to jump on them. His aunt often talked about everything's falling down "out there." He wasn't sure what the "out there" building-blocks were like, but he built more carefully than ever, trying to provide a calming antidote.

II

There was a lot of talk under the table, as the grown-ups kept each other happy during nights of particularly loud noises. Though he slept fitfully through much of it, it was here that he learned the beginnings of scientific enquiry, even philosophy.

One day, there was the rare appearance of a slight trace of butter, spread hesitantly on his evening slice of bread. Butter was rationed, though the government had found no way to ration how hungry they got. So he burst into tears when his slice fell onto the carpet, its buttered side down. His grandfather, and an uncle home on leave, sat themselves each side of him, and started a heated discussion, just to distract him. Their discussion held his attention like a large and firmly closed fist.

Grandfather maintained that bread always fell on carpets the butter-side down, throughout the entire universe, whatever planet you happened to be on at the time. It was a well known scientific law, that had held from the very beginning of everything, including butter, carpets and bread. Uncle Jed pointed out that "always" is a pretty big word, and that it should be put properly to the test, as scientists would do. (He had recently graduated from High School into the army.) Grandfather said that they would do an experiment using Uncle's half-eaten slice of bread. Would he kindly donate it for the purpose of genuine research?

The toddler watched in amazement, as Uncle Jed, with humour at war with the military sadness in his face, slowly opened his hand, and let his bread fall on the carpet. Then he shouted, victory in his voice, "Look, the bread's fallen butter-side up!" But grandfathers are never to be proven conclusively wrong. That's an even more fundamental law of the universe, whatever table you happen to be under at the time: "It only shows your mother buttered the wrong side of the bread." Grandfather then held forth on what would happen, anywhere in the universe, if a slice of bread were tied, butter-side up, to a willing cat's back. As cats always fall on their feet, the cat-plus-bread would drop to just above the floor, and spin there indefinitely, like a magical spinning top. The abstruse details of this argument were beyond a toddler, but the seeds of a lively interest in things being dropped were well sown, and the crying had stopped.

Shortly after the bread experiment, he had one of his few trips outside "house" during those many months of noisy nights. It gave him an opportunity to drop things in a different part of the universe than under a table, where, perhaps, entirely special conditions hold. His mother had just brought a large secondhand pram from a friend, with floorboards to it, under which she could store shopping. She wheeled it back from the friend's, doing a bit of shopping on the way. Wanting to celebrate the capture of a pram, she used up all her rationing coupons to buy a bar of chocolate, which was rarely sighted in those parts. She parked the pram by the side of the house, and put him in it for the unusual experience of a bit of fresh air. While she was inside, unpacking the shopping, he discovered the floorboards, edged one up, and found the forgotten chocolate.

Being an obedient child, he only chewed off three corners, but then was overwhelmed by questions. Which side up would it fall? Would it spin, like his brightly coloured top? Or could only a ginger-and-white-cat, with buttered bread attached, spin properly? He'd no sooner dropped the chocolate bar over the side of the pram, than there was a loud explosion, and the pram fell on its side, spilling him into the gutter. That's where his desperate mother found him, seconds later, shaking his small fists at the departing tail fins of a German bomber. It had dropped its bombs in a nearby empty field, either through a bent corkscrew of bad aim, or to conserve fuel for the long haul home. In later years, he thought that's where his pacifism began; also his tendency to find himself in the gutter just now and again. But isn't that how you learn things: in mixed packets? And it was years before he dared to eat chocolate again. At the time, he was so relieved to be returned to safety under the table. It was demonstrably the natural and proper place for people to live. Overweening pride and curiosity should never trick one beyond it.

III

One evening, just before the worst of the nights of noise, he had the rare treat of being taken into the garden. His mother had gone for the day to work in a distant "outside," with a strange red cross pinned to her sleeve. Auntie Doss was more prepared to be adventurous with him, and they sat under the plum-tree. She had just pointed out a tawny owl flying by in the dusk, when the air raid sirens began. He was intrigued to hear so clearly what had been muffled inside, under that table. The sirens slowly raised their wolves' heads, and howled into the cloudy sky. The howls hung there like long, metallic threads of tinsel, awaiting the rest of someone's Christmas or birthday decorations.

He expected his aunt to clutch him up, and run for the house. But she held him quietly in her lap, and seemed to know that what the wolves were howling at would stay some distance away. She remained quite calm, despite the excited sound of feet on the far side of the fence, as neighbours ran for the air raid shelter at the bottom of their garden. Their footsteps, in the fallen leaves, sounded like the soft but deliberate swirlings of a tap filling a bath. Grandfather had not thought it fitting to build a bomb shelter in his garden. He dug a marrow patch instead. In his reckoning, vegetable marrows beat bombs any day.

Then came the sound of the wings of a very large owl in flight. It must've been far, far bigger than the owl that had flown by them earlier. At first, the wings beat, but then began to shake, the air all around them. It was as if someone were shaking their whole garden like a doormat. His aunt pointed upwards, but all he could see were plums twirling on their stalks, as rapidly as his mother twirled around her happiness in her one summer dress. He wondered whether he'd be shaken like dust right off the doormat of the garden, but was reassured by his aunt's calm.

Long white fingers of light began to reach up into the sky. They were as spindly as his grandmother's fingers; but so white and ringless, that they seemed talcum-powdered and prepared for some rare special occasion. Not having seen them before, he didn't realize the occasion was now nightly. The fingers began to twitch and jerk across the sky, like grandmother's when she laughed. For him, unlike the adults, who understood consequences, it was all spectacle. But, without consequences, glorious spectacle, indeed, it was. Much later in life, he would still remember it as beautiful, though as a terrible beauty: a beauty that terrorized and demoralized itself.

The fingers of light reached higher and higher, grew longer and longer, thinner and thinner, until they were more like the filament-legs of a giant, many-legged insect, a spider perhaps, scissoring and striding across the sky, trying not to slip back into the black birdbath of the night, trying to get a grip. Sometimes the legs intersected and met, as though the insect had caught hold of something. Sometimes the searchlights revealed a barrage balloon, much like the great, grey, creased backside of the elephant in one of his picture books. Only these elephants, even better than in the story, were part of a marvelous flying circus.

Ack-ack guns started, their tracers arcing upwards, like rice-grains on fire from his grandmother's burned rice pudding. With guns nearer at hand, the shining tracers were more like his bag of clear marbles, flung out and up in a row. There was such a variety of noises, that he'd only heard muffled together from under the table: the wing-beats and hooting roars of gigantic owls, the garden shaken like a rug that would soon fray and fall apart from the effort, the ack-ack guns like huge dogs that could only stutter when they barked, the howls of the wolf-head sirens still raised to the sky. Voices shouted things like "Coming in at 2-o-clock." In this setting, even the spider-legs in the sky seemed to stride with their own silvery sibilance.

Then came the sound of the bombs. They were so loud, he soon could hear nothing, had gone temporarily deaf. But he could see the branches of the plum tree swaying above them, and the tree twist around its own trunk. He knew that sound had been transposed into pure motion. Later, he would remember the tree, twisting around its trunk, as like a chicken desperately trying to wring its own neck. They couldn't directly see what the bombs had done. The moon kept its face turned sorrowfully away, behind the clouds. But in the distance, towards the centre of the city, they could see large tomcats' tongues of fire lapping at clouds of dust, as though these were pools of rationed milk turned an even dirtier grey than usual.

He slept well that night, back under the table, in the crook of his mother's arm. It was the sleep of those who don't know the consequences. He would learn them soon enough.

IV

About a week later, the noise outside was different. The pre-historic pterodactyls of steel were flying directly overhead. He could tell, from the way the candle flame and the black-out curtains shimmied in a downdraft from the chimney. The fireless hearth sucked and blew air eagerly, making a sound like an excited mouth organ. But there were no loud explosions. However, there were sounds from the top of the house, as if his grandfather were hard at it again in the attic, hammering nails and at least three thumbs, and had thrown both the hammer and a very large bag of nails onto the floor. But only he, his mother and father, were at home; and they were where all good people should definitely be: under the dining room table.

His father, whether driven by fate, or freed by chance, happened to be on leave from the front on the night of the incendiary bombing. In later years, he thought his father most probably freed fate into chance on most occasions, as he was unbeatable at cards, and called out "Lady Luck!" successfully most times when he rolled the dice. His parents ran up the stairs to the attic, and he clambered slowly behind. On previous rare visits, he'd been as enchanted by the attic as it had been by him. It was cluttered with draped silhouettes that had intrigued him as much as coming across a herd of pit-ponies at the top of the stairs—the herd his grandfather often talked about—all grazing quietly under their long horse blankets. In his sleep, that attic was full of silhouetted and comforting dreams, which he slowly uncovered there. But tonight, the attic was not the source of quietly grazing dreams.

He hung back a floor below, by the bathroom door with his mother, as his father rushed into the attic to face a monstrous crackling rat that had intruded. It completely filled the room. It had pushed steel-hardened whiskers and nose through the roof, and its jaws and eyes splayed fire. When he was older, he connected this sight with words from the book of Lamentations: "That thy cities be laid waste," "And burn, burn, that none can quench it." At the time, though, it was, entirely, Rat incarnate. By fate, or chance, a rusty bucket appeared in his father's hand (there was still probably a pair of dice in his pocket), and he ran down to the bathroom to fill it. Bucket in hand, his father fought Rat hard. But he was clawed back rapidly, having to run down one floor each time, to refill the bucket under an interminably slow-running and traitorous tap. He left the tap running, the water pattering away down the plug-hole to its own air raid shelter somewhere in the basement.

At this point, he saw his mother push the perished, rubber, snot-smelling plug into the plug-hole, so that the bath began at least to imagine it might gather water, though not fill with it. She did this with her eyes very deliberately lowered, and kept them down afterwards, not looking at anything in particular. He thought this odd, as a toddler. Grown-ups had to look down when under the table, as there was no room to look up. So they usually looked anywhere but down when they could stand, stretching and rubbing their necks like giraffes freed from the confines of his picture-book. But it was her way of being discreet and not "Why can't you do things properly!" with his father, even in this battle for survival. His father made increasingly desperate forays upstairs to the attic. Now able to fill the bucket almost faster than immediately from the tub, he forced Rat back, thumbnail by blackened thumbnail, by singed airman's moustache. Below, the tub was seen to wobble—or was it dance excitedly?—on its gryphon-taloned feet. His mother encouraged it, and joined in unobtrusively, when his father's back was turned.

V

Despite being up most of the night, they were awoken at dawn by the chirping of a cocksparrow in the attic, who'd flown in through the hole in the roof. It was overjoyed not to have fallen from its nest in the eaves the night before, in the last hallelujahs of a charred song. His father returned to the front a few days later, with a new and unopened pack of cards. The nights of noise came less and less often, and then stopped altogether. The iron decrees of fate seemed to be losing out to the delighted luck of the draw under the many tables and kitchen sinks throughout the country. Their airmen had been dealt some good hands among the difficult ones, and had played them well. His grandfather harvested a giant marrow that had outlived and out-swollen all the bombs, and they ate well at last.

Eventually, the momentous day came when they took that giant step for their kind, and emerged from under-the-table-life to live in the house, and even go outside. When he thought of it later, it was like the first walking fish, that crawled from beneath the slow rhythms of those floating mats of seaweed that swirl in the tide, to live among the faster rhythms of land. Some of the adjustments took time, such as walking about without the reassuring and somewhat splintered tousling of your hair on the underneath of a table. There was much, too, that he carried into later life from that earlier one. He was often struck by how, paradoxically, the smallest details in people's behaviour may have the biggest significance. After all, there's not much choice but to notice small details, when growing up with others under the dining room table. In particular, he realized, early on, the many ways in which a woman's seemingly deferential, though quietly authoritative and untrembling small hand, can triumph over furies that would otherwise go forth in the land. However, never discount the emphasis given to a father's actions by his rotating the knuckles of a closed hand. Even if that hand is empty of dice, Lady Luck is just waiting to be conjured up, too.

The Banjo Case

Not so long ago, though it keeps getting longer, some young children lived in a small village in the south of England. They were utterly remarkable, but only to themselves. Peace had just been declared at the end of the Second World War. The village itself had had no strategic importance in the recent events; unless to scavenging foxes, their shoulder blades as sharp as coat hangers, who had their own hard time of it when chickens became scarce. The horse trough in front of the bakery was clearly indefensible; and the seat round the bottom of the elm had no more treasure buried beneath it, after one of the children picked up a bent and very skinny penny.

A long tricycle ride from the elm tree, and you would probably need an apple to eat on the way back, lay the flat and grassy fields used by the planes. Bombers had taken off from there at night, usually returning well before morning. The children didn't see them often, though they heard them from their beds, and watched their curtains shimmying with the noise. Their questions were discouraged. The bombers had gradually come to seem like big iron bees, buzzing cavernously to something distant that interested them; frightening, but as natural as other night time insects. Then things changed. The grown-ups all became much happier. Events took a dramatic turn for the better. The children found this disturbing. Was it only they who noticed?

Before, if the children had been up late, and caught sight of a line of black bombers clambering up over the tousled tops of the trees, they had instinctively looked away. It was something you wanted to watch, like a rabbit dangling from the blades of a harvesting machine, its twitching back reshaped as a triangle; but something you couldn't watch for long. Though the iron bees were carrying their stings elsewhere, their dull drone filled the sky above the village with the sure promise that, somewhere, field after field of rabbits would be dangling and stiffening soon; and more than rabbits too.

Now, with peace declared, the bombers only landed. They never seemed to take off. It went on for weeks. There were more bombers, and of more different kinds, than the children had ever seen. This was the first thing to alert them; though the grown-ups seemed happier than ever before, and continually going to parties when it was no one's birthday. That bombers landed without having taken off, had all the disturbing features of things coming down that had never gone up. It was as though hundreds of balls just kept tumbling down out of the elm trees, when none of the children had thrown one up.

Something else that alerted the children was that the planes came in during the daylight, right before your eyes. Mothers, aunts and grandmothers, who, during night-time flying, had fairly quickly looked away, now eagerly nailed their eyes onto the incoming specks, pointing and waving. And the planes were no longer at all shy about being seen. They came in lazily, waggling their wing-tips over the village, even circling it, before dropping out of sight below the hedgerows. The older children learned to point and wave too. But the four-year-olds pushed up against their mothers' aprons, or ran inside with the even younger ones. Iron bees were still clearly iron bees, even if they waggled in the sunshine.

As remnants of bomber squadrons returned from various outposts of war, using the airfield as a staging point, the sky was in a continual uproar. Some of the children began, nervously, to play further afield. It was a bit of a novelty. Thunder kept coming out of a cloudless sky, and no rain fell. None of them noticed any lightning at first, either. That came later. They got used to the thunder, without actually liking it. They no longer had to screw their eyes shut, fingers poked firmly in their ears. They began to notice things that the grown-ups couldn't, being so busy indoors with their birthday parties.

If you were playing by a wall when the thunder came, the wall seemed to shout back to other nearby walls. Then they would all go hoarse in a pounding hubbub together. But the well shouted only to itself. The shout went round and round inside it, and got sucked down the shaft to the water at the bottom. You could tell when it had finished swallowing its shout. That was when the water began to wobble. The well got rid of a lot of thunder that way. In this respect, it was a good place to play by, though otherwise strictly forbidden. A particularly deep rumbling overhead drove ripples across the horse trough and ponds. The ripples were shaped like long spiked nails. None of the children had seen ripples like that before.

Occasionally, the drumming in the sky was built into their games. It could make balls of spit bounce across cobblestones, just like beads of milk spilt on the stove. To win, your spit had to bounce right across the road, into a flower bed opposite. The most difficult part was its hopping the curb, but it could do that too. The boys got some laughs from how the girls' cotton dresses kept trembling on them, even when the girls stood quite still. The girls were called "scaredies" and, later, "scaredy-planes". But that was only until some of the girls noticed how the boys' shirtsleeves were just as agitated, in the rarer moments when the boys were still. After the first few weeks, it was almost possible to shut out the clattering roar, as another line of bombers climbed down through the ravens and tree tops. Instead, the children developed a nervous interest in seeing what new things the sound could do as it got loose in the village.

Returning airmen strolled into the village, on the path that came out by the elm tree. Some of them talked a bit funny. Nearly all of them walked with a stiff bounce that came in mid-stride. That was like the jerk and then push of a clockwork train, when it hasn't been played with all summer, and the spring needs oiling. As with the trains, it soon wore off. The seat round the elm was usually packed with pilots. There was plenty of treasure there again, as they gave away chocolate and chewing gum, but no bent pennies. When they first arrived, they liked dancing in the street by the bakery. Even the grandmothers danced with them. But they soon settled down, and spent hours just sitting and listening to the leaves above them. They talked quietly among themselves, and wrestled matches constantly in and out of clusters of pipes, looking up when the next line of planes came into view. After a while, people didn't look up much any more. Only Mrs. Deakes did, and put on her red skirt.

Once, an airman piggy-backed one of the boys to the airfield, to show him some planes. Otherwise, that was out-of-bounds. Afterwards, the boy said how, walking on wing-tips that no longer wiggled, the covers of the cockpits looked full of clouds. When you stuck your head inside, you could smell that lightning had struck there many, many times. The skies themselves, however, remained clear and blue, as if clouds drifted by only in bombers now.

After two weeks of nearly daily dancing in the streets, the mothers quietened down too. But the dancing went on in the front of their eyes. Perhaps that was why they didn't see what was happening, though the smallest children could. It wasn't surprising they failed to notice how spit could bounce. At their age, mothers can be presumed to have run out of spit anyway; or they spit in a terrible hurry, just to get done with it, and don't stay to watch. But much was afoot in their house-proud homes, right under their noses. However, as some of the children remembered it afterwards, the changes in the houses took place after the changes outside. It seemed to be spreading inwards.

The first thing that happened was that the house cats all disappeared. Some of them were seen walking together into the fields. Even cats who usually fought each other like demons went silently side by side. They didn't run, but put their paws down firmly in front of them, to show something was on their minds. Later, they were found to have joined the farm cats, but only in the most distant and broken-down barns.

Inside the houses, the battering roar of the bombers was a little muted, especially in the older cottages, with stone walls wide enough to keep summer out and winter in all the year round. But even there, things started up. You might be sitting at table, sometimes with even your eyes dribbling as the food was brought in. Though food got rationed, no one had thought to make belly-growls take it in turns. As you grabbed the soup tureen with both your eyes, you could see how the thin broth sent up curiously separate little puffs of steam, as though it was panting anxiously. The more the planes landed, the more anxious the soups got.

Not long after the soup started panting, soot began to travel down chimneys. As it happened, the whole village had had its chimneys swept not long before, as the sweep from town did his rounds through the countryside. At first, only the finest powder fell. Later, huge crusts and lumps tumbled out on the hearthrugs. Mothers and aunts certainly noticed these. They grumbled as they cleared up the mess; talking to their knees as usual, to stop them getting cold on the flagstones. But the next moment, they were in a fresh dress, and off to the bakery, for dances or even bread. It didn't seem to strike them as odd that just-swept chimneys could shower down centuries of soot. After a while, the chimneys slowed down, but each day they scattered fresh black scabs on the floor. It was as though the chimneys had all hurt themselves badly, and kept bleeding inside. It went on for so long, that the children wondered whether their hearths would ever heal.

Once, one of the children left her crayons on the kitchen table for a whole day, lying about on some paper. By supper time, the crayons had scribbled a view from her life that made everything look as thin and as tangled-up as an abandoned ball of string. To the children, it was clear that something had shaken itself loose in the village, and could not be tightened up again. Peace and the safe return of the airmen had done what war, somehow distant from their village, had not. The children sensed that when their own fathers, who were sailors not airmen, returned, the men would notice the changes no more than the mothers had done. It was possible that the smell of lightning would come back with them too, stuck to the bottoms of their heavy boots together with the smell of occasional dogs and the sea. Those whose fathers returned turned out right about that.

Today, those events in the village are over fifty years ago. But no one seems to have reported them yet. Perhaps it is too late now for things to be reversed. As it happens, I was one of those children. I can still remember my grandpa's banjo case, propped against the wall in the cold front room. My brother and I were forbidden to touch that banjo, while grandpa was away at sea. The instrument leant there, nonchalant as a sailor, waiting for him to come back and half-sing, half-roar as usual, after supper, to help my grandma get the dishes clean. She would sing too, in a light and floating voice that sounded full of sunny soap bubbles from the sink.

One day, towards the end of the time of the bombers' return, my three-year-old brother and I found ourselves promisingly alone in the house. Hauled along by the gravitational force of the forbidden, we met in the front room, beside the banjo. The room was forbidden too, except on Sundays, and when accompanied by an adult. It was filled with an ormolu clock, a glass case full of shepherdesses and commemorative mugs, and one giant spider that swung commandingly in the perpetually unlit fireplace. I already had the banjo case laid across my knees, easing out the straps, when the shepherdesses suddenly began to shift and rotate on their shelves, crooks rattling loudly. This was to be expected, and left us undeterred. It was merely another squadron of bombers lowering themselves in. Then, with horror, we heard the faint sounds of strings being stirred inside the nearly opened banjo case.

We ran to the door we had so carefully closed to avoid easy detection. But before we could reach it, the varnish-darkened door gave a heave and shake, like a black bull irritated by flies, and slowly shuddered open. We could hear floorboards beyond it creaking with heavy footsteps. We looked at each other in chilled desperation. We were both quite sure that grandpa, in the unutterable wisdom of his wild black beard, had somehow anticipated the exact moment of our misdeed, and run invincibly across the stormy wave-tops from his ship, to take charge of the banjo and stop us.

Frantic not to be discovered, and not to meet grandpa in a moment when his remarkable powers were quite so fully revealed, we ran to the open window, and lobbed ourselves through. It was actually a blessed relief to land among the erect spears and drawn knives of the prize rose garden.

An hour later, after circling round the house with extreme caution, past the coal bunker, over the apple tree, under drenched ferns and foxgloves, we found no trace of anyone at home. In fact, we never encountered grandpa again. His body was found, covered with oil, drifting three miles from where his battle-broken ship had foundered in the Irish Sea. By the time the last bombers were landing, it was clear to my brother and me, on legitimate Sunday visits to the front room, that the banjo strings had retuned themselves to a different and more jangling pitch than grandpa would ever have approved.

I have the banjo in its case beside me now, an ocean and almost a lifetime away from that village. Somehow, I never learned to play it, though I play several other instruments. Wherever I moved across the world, the sound of strings being stirred by a stealthy hand went on steadily. It made no difference whether I was living beside quivering truck routes or in quiet backwoods. Lately, though, or so it seems to me, the noise has been getting louder. The dog has started looking at the case inquiringly, teeth at least half at the ready. I must put the banjo up in the roof before our guests come to stay this weekend. An increasingly uneven music is playing, playing.

Sea Changes

A clock

Just after the war—a clock on the sea-facing wall of a cabin by the shore.
It had a clown-face dial, with wide eyes moving from side
to side, as the pendulum swung. Those eyes neither blinked
nor closed, though the boy watched patiently. What else to do,
when it rained? His father, just de-mobbed, often slept in a rocking chair
that wouldn't rock, since a runner was loose. But his Dad's eyes lurched
ceaselessly, behind closed lids, presumably on runners of their very own.
What he dreamed of refused to dismantle into some done-for and
stationary past.

Twice a day, when the tide turned, candles on the table
flickered uncertainly, in those dark winter months. Twice
a day, the tongue in his father's mouth also wavered, in a drafty
bluster of words, uncertain whether to curse or bless the universe.
Twice a day, the clock on the sea-surged wall stopped,
in synchronized sympathy. Its large eyes now motionless, the clown
no longer seemed to smile, but stared in a crazed suspended judgement.

Something on the beach

Something ahead on the beach, with a crowd of people around it.
Too late to make a detour, as they'd just turned the corner of a cove.
Out for a walk with his parents, he held on like a limpet to his mother's
hand.
A sailor's cap and naval kit bag had been cast up
on the turn of the tide. That must be a drowned seaman beside them,
draped
in tightly coiled bladder-wrack and immaculate black
ribbons of tar. A coast guard lifted up one
of the sailor's hoofs gently. Another raised the head
until a snout pointed straight at the sky, with shining curved
tusks just below. The tide was going out very quickly
because of the smell, vomiting thick spray over rock pools.
"Pigs are hopelessly bad swimmers," his father said.
"But what a sod the sea is, to dress it up like a man."
Flies braided themselves into thick mooring ropes on their faces.
The boy crushed a handful. They turned into drops of tar
and dripped back onto the pig-sailor. The tide went out
more and more quickly, unconcerned, as is natural, about anything
but itself.

The father's parable of the pig-sailor

I remember walking back to that cove in the evening, on my own, when our son was asleep. The pig-sailor was still there, though cap and kitbag had been removed, I assume by the military police. The creature swayed back and forth, crouching. Then it humped up and down, energetic with a heaving black undulation of flies. It was just bristling and matted with them. It twitched with an electric vitality, humming as loudly as an exposed high voltage cable. It was clearly in some kind of majestic, rippling prime, intent on its own hungry purposes: mating, perhaps, or hunting, or finding a whole pack of its species. —Whatever its needs were, and I didn't want to know.

Though I stood very carefully upwind, I could smell something peculiarly like sulphur. It eyed me through eerily eyeless but attentively flickering sockets, whose gaze crawled right through you. It seemed one creature entire in its unfathomable prancing intent. Without warning, it lurched toward me. Or did something slip and gave way? At the time, I wasn't sure which. At any rate, I suddenly felt sharply noticed: part of a plan, or, more likely, a swarming chaos. It felt too much like meeting Lucifer himself, just cast to earth from heaven, or from the depths to dry land, on a tide one way or the other, and bitterly resenting his punishment.

I watched as the sea came in to reclaim its own. The tide gives, then the tide takes away. Then the tide gives back, somewhere else, some of its take-away. Reluctant flies left solo, then in groups, as the approaching spray harassed them. Lucifer's single prancing intent gradually broke up, streaming off in all directions, going wherever it is random gusts take blowflies. Is Lucifer ever more than that, d'you think, some mindless and innumerable multitude: our small acts taken cumulatively, so difficult to contend with and change because there are just so many of them?

In the kitchen

For supper, if the catch was good, they ate shrimp and potato.
His father strode into the kitchen, galoshes slurping thirstily
with what sounded like all eight of the seven seas. A full net
squirmed beneath his hand. He tipped the still-twitching shrimps
into a pan of water already teased to a boil of fast-rolling
anticipation on the stove. The shrimps leapt straight out
again, like squibs exploding in every direction. Most fell back in,
antennae as bent and smashed as barley stalks after a storm.

But a few always managed to fly on in an arc: changed, suddenly,
into a flock of pink and be-whiskered, flipper-tailed birds.

If his father had been particularly lucky in searching the rock pools,
he would pry mussel shells open. Then short tongues
lolled out of each, floppily, still trying to recite
the name, rank and number of both incoming and outgoing tides.

What you can learn from a well

One day, I showed our small son where the old well is. It's all overgrown with brambles, beside the cabin. My father got me and my two brothers to dig it, years ago. We were part boys imagining ourselves men, and, when it suited us, part men imagining ourselves boys again. We played double agents a lot with time, then. Can't do that anymore. Now, if you take the cover off, the well's only drunk at by the brown hedge that leans over it. The hedge more or less grows out of its own reflection, as the soil is so poor here. Seawind mutters though that hedge without ever stopping to catch its breath. The well tries to stay pretty unnoticed: I'm just here to serve you. But, like all wells, it's seen and knows a lot.

At the top, we made a ledge to store butter in the summer. Though it got beaded with sweat from the water below. In the water at the bottom, we found old bones, but smoothed and softened into such anonymous slivers, you couldn't tell what species they belonged to: a hawk, a lamb, a fish, perhaps a man, even a hawkman or a lamb-fish. Gave me the odd feeling that, in the biggest picture of all, it doesn't matter which particular species you get born into. The real difference is between being here as a something or other, and not being born at all. Underneath, we're all just very ambivalent slivers of life. At the Front, I reckon we were hawks or wolves as much as we were men. Life's an awfully flexible operator.

Below the mud at the bottom—as we know from digging there—there's only hard rock, saying all that rock has ever learned to say: that it's damned hard rock. Formed by tireless volcanic fires that view us people as late, minor and rather short-lived obstacles to their own splendid, long term progress. Rock that might've been, but for the accidents of gravity, rock on a distant planet, coursing where my father and two brothers were never born; where wells were never dug or imagined; where our father never rewarded us each with a pint and a shilling.

Anyway, after a few years, we had to stop using the well. Its water got saltier and saltier. The same unalterable tides move down there as are in the bay, and—so it seems—down the whole course of history. Wherever we are, we're all being washed around in the same big sea.

The Church of Unredeemable Spray

The first winter after the war was one of very bad storms.
Huge swells trained their siege-guns on the sea wall.
Could we ever make peace with the waters too? It seemed doubtful.
As swell hit the wall, it ricocheted as a vast, reversed,
rampant waterfall, right over the Church of St. Mark:
henceforth to be known, in the chronicles, as the Church of
    Unredeemable Spray.
Organ pipes breathed salt glitters of glissandos.
Stained glass windows became sides of a pea-green aquarium,
with small fish shoaling incuriously through each station of the Cross.
Memorial tiles tried hard to save the remembrance
of women and children first. Even the spire began to tilt
its lumbering mast, making heavy weather of any certainty.
Wherever the horizon was now, it heaved-ho in complete indifference
to our Sunday need to know what's above, what's far below.

How to swim-climb a tree

The boy was hopeless at tree climbing, though he kept on trying,
on the old holm-oak by the cabin, that we had thought was dying
even when I helped dig the well. Then, one day,
when a rough sea was, as usual, swaggering around and smashing
things
on the beach, I looked out the window, and saw something happen
to him.
As a particularly big wave crashed onto the beach, he suddenly
changed his stance, and skimmed along a branch in fluid movements,
as though swimming up out of that wave; his head tilted
back, eyes fixed as if on some surface-light above,
pupils so enlarged they could easily buoy him after them, catching
every bit of phosphorescence in the strange evening light.
He cast off up that tree, rather than climbed it, as nimble as a bubble.

A walled garden

One Friday, his mother wanted a few groceries from the village. She peddled a large wicker basket attached to an inconspicuous bicycle, and took her son with her, in the basket, both for company and for ballast. The road into the village was a-swirl, flooded with sea spray, and she couldn't get through. Luckily, a gardener on the land side of the road spotted her, and let them into the shelter of a walled garden. Here, the heavy artillery of the sea, its quick-firing cannonades of colliding waves, the ack-ack of scared dogs' yaps, the screaming buckshot of blown gulls' cries, were muffled. Layer after layer of moss grew on each other, until they forgot that they were meant to be attached to anything beyond themselves. After a breather, the gardener let them out of another gate, further back up the road, and they returned to the cabin. He waved as they cycled away. He stroked a fish-shaped moustache with one hand. A grey cascade from his shoulders was desperately trying to turn back into a raincoat.

Going shopping by kayak

When his mother wheeled her basket back into the cabin, his father decided to go shopping by kayak, and paddle along the shore to the village. Seas weren't running that high. The trouble on land seemed mostly with windblown spray. Beside, his weekly order of baccy desperately needed him. The boy went with him, as he often did in the big, thick hulled sea kayak.

They made a quick, safe trip to the store. On the way back, the tide turned strangely, just off the cabin. The paddle slipped and careened through what felt like sudden vacuums and big bubbles of air below. Then, the next moment, it dragged to a standstill, as if stuck in molasses or a pot of cooling tar. Foam seemed to curdle on the lifted blades, and their grip in the sea quickly decayed and went rancid. The harder his father paddled towards the cabin, the further they were carried out to sea.

It was then that they spotted a seal swimming nearby, head raised high. Its grey coat streamed with stormy light, as though it might, at any moment, turn, without remainder, into the broodiest of weather. It seemed to be watching them. Every so often, a flipper was raised to place a moustache-shaped fish in its mouth, just below its bristling whiskers. At first, the boy, tired by now, half-wondered whether it might, half-possibly, be the gardener. The seal kept swimming out into a choppy maelstrom of water, then coming back beside them, as if urging them to follow.

At last, the boy's father followed. He'd looked at his son, now swaying trustfully asleep between his knees in the kayak's foam-and-sweat-flecked cockpit. If a wave can teach a boy how to climb trees, where's it written that a seal can't guide you home? Anyway, he'd tried everything else, and the cabin was drifting further and further off. Once into that choppy circle of water, the outward current eased off. His blades took good, even bites out of the waves. They were soon back at the cabin, escorted close to shore by the seal.

Later that evening

Later that evening, Mom noticed, with surprise, that, at this particular turn of the tide, the clown-faced clock hadn't stopped at all. With its eyes darting from side to side, it smiled as companionably as any clock can. She'd fixed both her petticoat and the runner of the rocking chair while they'd been out in the kayak, with all of the precision of a recent munitions worker. Dad dozed in the chair, rocking gently. The boy was curious that there were moments when his father's eyes, unexpectedly, didn't lurch at all behind their closed lids.

Underneath Things

After breakfast, Nikos stood by the front door, wondering what to do with a Saturday free of school and chores. He began to walk, following his feet with his usual open-mindedness, to see where they'd go. The early morning light was as grey as the bread dough his mother had just put in the oven; and mist ladled itself over the sea like a cold, thin porridge. Rain would surely come later.

He found himself by the shed where what was left of his father's fishing tackle was stored. His father had been lost at sea before he was born, but rolled nets still waited patiently for him. Nikos pulled out an air rifle from under some sacking, together with a box of pellets, then stapled a new target to the door. The door was as pockmarked and scarred as a desperado's face. That was from the target practice of his uncle Kostas, fifteen years before. It was Kostas's old gun. His uncle was away in the army on the mainland now, serving as a sharpshooter.

Nikos stepped back twenty paces, and looked carefully down the gun-sights. He must allow for the deflection of the wind, the birdsong, and unseen crickets all around him, sawing the air into finer and finer woodchips, then into sheer sawdust. There was also the much greater deflecting force of the dark brown eyes of the girl next door, Tula, as she watched him, while hanging out her mother's washing: different coloured panties for each day of the week. He must allow, too, for the tilt of the hillside lane running beside him. Even the handlebars of his bike twitched with anxiety on that lane, when speed gathered him eagerly to itself, his bell ringing in frantic mid-air all on its own.

He squeezed off shots carefully for well over an hour, one after another. A constant stream of armed and belligerent insurgents, from every century of military history, passed conveniently in front of the frontlines of the shed door. They sometimes got their centuries mixed up. Roman legionnaires held a last stand against him, manning machine-guns. Paratroopers floated down on 'chutes, then threw spears at him. The day grew warmer. He felt at the very centre of it. As though he were being narrated, as the main character in a story, by a storyteller hidden behind the furthest olive tree.

Unexpectedly, the storyteller related an old woman down the lane, walking to market. She was dressed all in black, "like a lonely crow" as the hidden storyteller put it. She was related past Nikos with a limp and red socks. She waved at him. The day grew warmer still. It was nearly noon. "Then Pavli came up the hill with his goats, seeking cooler ground. His flock was neverending." Nikos listened, with pleasure, to the story in his head. And neighbour Pavli appeared, on cue, his huge flock of goats flowing on and on into the shade of the olive trees. After that, in Nikos's opinion, the story faltered, more description than action. A cloud of dust got itself floatingly recounted high up into the air from the goats' hooves, full of the smell of goat droppings, crushed thistles and freshly baked bread. Church bells started ringing through the middle of the cloud.

Tired of having his day narrated, Nikos walked over to the target, to see how accurate his aim had really been. He'd managed to hit the bull's-eye, at its edges, six times. That bull would never blink again. Counting things helped him step out of a story when he wanted to. The target was in tatters, with his crinkly-edged lead pellets embedded in its thick cardboard. He tore it off the shed-door, to put a new one in its place. It was then that he noticed a cluster of smooth-edged pellets embedded in the door itself, right at the centre of where his bull's-eye had been. They must be Kostas's, from fifteen years before. They were certainly rust-streaked. He felt beaten. With that last target, Kostas had been by far the best shot. He put up a new target, trying to pick a spot where Kostas's pellets were not much in evidence.

He allowed himself ten carefully placed shots, and then stepped up to the target again. That was better: three at the edges of the bull's-eye. He felt at the centre of things again. But then, abruptly, things were told very vividly, from beyond the washing line of brightly coloured panties, from beyond the furthest olive tree, with an unexpected turn. "Yet, when he looked under the target, what did he see ..." Nikos peeled back the target, only to find that Kostas had beaten him again, easily.

Nikos kept trying, with new targets, each time selecting a different part of the door. Surely, it was just chance that he'd found Kostas's pellets under the bull's-eyes so far. But, every single time, Kostas beat him, hands down. The day got warmer still. He began to do worse and worse. The rasping of crickets, and Tula's more and more insistent gaze, spun his senses and pellets wide of the shed. An old crow was recapitulated back up the road from the market, red socks now slipping down over her heels. This time, he waved back, though he'd had it drummed into him at school that listeners to stories are only ever supposed to listen.

The spell of the story was weakening. Nikos slipped back to the edge, not the centre, of things. Not even the edge. How can you be at an edge, among gnarled olive trees, unless you know where the centre is? He followed his feet once more, to see where they'd lead him. This time, he had to run to keep up with them, past the furthest olive tree to the small tavern-cum-store. Old Angelos was sitting outside at the table, entertaining a small group of wine glasses and a single crony. The glasses looked empty, his friend looked full. His voice drifted over as Nikos approached.

"Pavli's goats were all old in my grandfather's time. They stand in that shade, year after year, summer into winter. There's always the same number of them. They keep renewing themselves, somehow, from the clouds of dust they raise, and from the constant church bells, especially around Easter. Pavli rehashes himself, too. Even if I have to say it again: my grandfather swore his own grandfather knew Pavli."

Nikos sat at the curb, listening. He reached for a stick lying nearby, and began to whittle it with his pocket knife. Slivers of wood hailed though the air and scattered around him. Angelos looked at him out of the corner of his eye, smiled to himself mischievously, and went on talking. "And you've seen the crook Pavli carries. He whittles away at it to pass the time, every day. He has no wife to whittle away at, no sons to carve his name in. But that crook never gets smaller. Under each sliver, there's exactly the same crook as before. Amazing what you can find underneath things." Nikos looked at his stick. It was hard, dry wood. His wrist was tired. The stick looked bigger than before. He threw it across the road.

Angelos's face was covered with tanned and weathered wrinkles. Even the wrinkles had wrinkles on top of them. Nikos asked himself whether you should trust a man with so many wrinkles. After all, where had they all come from? At ten years old, he had absolutely no idea. Angelos smiled his lopsided smile, and the wrinkles tilted without warning. A passing cyclist rang his bell in non-stop alarm, and sped by recklessly. Nikos wondered whether the crooked wrinkles spilled out from an equally large number of crooked thoughts. Was Angelos's brain remaking itself all over his face?

Angelos waved his now empty wine glass at Nikos. "Nikos, you're mother's gone down to the harbour. The mail packet's come in. There may be news from your uncle Kostas. What a crack shot that man is! He can pick off a rabbit half-an-hour after noon, without nicking its shadow." Nikos picked up his stick again, and walked away, heading for his house. Angelos's voice kept up with him easily. It had very long legs. It followed him even beyond earshot of where Angelos sat by the tavern. Nikos was not surprised at this. Obviously, it wanted to see where his feet would lead them both. What else can you expect from so many wrinkles? The voice went on. It was stereophonic: both in his head and, back at the tavern, beyond the furthest olive tree. "The day grew still warmer. Pavli stood in the shade with his neverending flock. The sea was blue and always rediscovering itself." When Nikos passed by the shepherd, he was careful not to wave to him. If he was listening properly, Pavli must be left undisturbed.

Nikos stood by the front door of his house, looking down at the bay and the sea. Rainclouds rumbled high up, like approaching squadrons of bombers, positioning themselves carefully. The sea heaved knowingly. From this height, it looked wrinkled all over with the glint of waves. For Nikos, it was not so much a view, as an ancient character in a story. He often waited to see what it would do next. But, like Tula hanging out her seven young colours of panties, the sea had done nothing yet, except look right back at him.

Nikos was surprised to find the door locked. Still, these were uncertain times, as uncle Kostas often wrote in his letters. His mother would have left the key under the flower pot, perhaps with a note for him. But there was only a silk-white mushroom growing under the pot, with a crushed snail beside it. Back at the tavern, as if on cue, Angelos began re-telling one of his favourite stories. He was beyond earshot, but Nikos listened anyway. Why not? There was nothing else to do. A new crowd was gathering.

"Huge white mushrooms fell out of the sky. Do you remember May the twentieth, 1941? They multiplied and billowed as they fell. Then we saw paratroopers dangling from them. Two Australians, with one machine-gun, made a salad of that first platoon. My grandfather helped later, with a pitchfork. Those mushroom-parachutes laid themselves out on the hillside, rippling peacefully. It was the first time, on this island, that children didn't want even a quick peep under things. A pair of very still, black German boots stuck out from each one. Later, more boots arrived, but this time they kept marching."

Nikos looked in the front window of their house, hands cupped to shade the glass. All he could see was a framed family photograph hanging on the damp wall opposite. His father and Kostas, as boys about his own age, stared back at him calmly, together with his grandparents. Their reserved expressions gave nothing away, except that they were being looked right through by an annoyingly undistractible recording photographer. "Who's always standing by some door, or behind an olive tree—and he likes his drink, too." A fragment of Angelos's next story wove in suddenly.

When Nikos looked at the picture, their expressions were unchanging. Nikos knew where he stood with his forebears. As Kostas had told him, the day he was called up, brushing cigarette ash off his new epaulettes, "Your father would want you to study hard at school. Be consistent. And practice each day with that gun." But when his mother came home, expressions in the family pictures would change. When she came in, giggling and smiling, with a new length of dress material, a gift from her admirer, the flatulent old tailor, relatives in the pictures seemed to mill about, even trade places. Some pictures in the room may have smiled with her, but others definitely frowned. The room either got bigger, or a whole lot smaller and more uncomfortable. When she came home tired-out from grape picking, inhabitants of the older pictures frowned with her, and promptly fell fast asleep, even while still dangling in their frames.

All the same, Nikos knew that, whatever the pictures felt for his mother, changing their moods, with hers, like the weather, when spring cleaning started, there'd be the same unchanged dark squares on the wall behind them, when she lifted them down. Even for his mercurial mother, there was this constancy, that couldn't be dusted or mopped away. And in the middle of each unchangeably dark square of the past, was the same self-replicating big spider, its head, even its eyes, as lined as Angelo's face.

Nikos cupped his hands more tightly to the window. The photograph seemed to straighten itself on the wall. He saluted back, brushing the first rain off his future epaulettes. A tractor cleared its throat and coughed in the lane, as if about to say something. Nikos saw Angelos approaching through the olive trees, walking so very slowly, he might as well have been trying to walk backwards. Usually, Angelos was swept swiftly onwards by his bushy grey beard. But, now, he squeezed it tightly in both hands, like a thin and essential handbrake.

Even beyond earshot, Nikos could hear him talking, right beside his head. "I'll tell the whole story. But it must take its own good time. You can't hurry a story." Angelos walked more and more slowly. He talked more and more diffidently. This was a story that was uncertain about telling itself. At a bend in the path, Angelos abruptly turned into the story, and stood as stock still as any blacksmith's anvil. But his lips went on moving. Confused, Nikos could take in only the sound of his voice. Carefully rounded syllables revolved awkwardly in Angelos's mouth, like large, hardboiled eggs, with bits of shell still attached. His lips fumbled their way, as though burned by spiced onions.

The rain fell more heavily. Copper pans in the house glowed darkly behind Nikos's back, a row of red and dented suns. A horse galloped by in the lane, trying to catch up with the tractor, the glitter of an unrisen moon in its eye, in the lessening light. Angelos came up to Nikos hesitantly, and put both hands on his shoulders. Nikos stepped back, embarrassed. No proper story should do that. "Nikos, your Uncle Kostas is dead. A notification came. Your mother is down in the harbour with the priest."

"Then the boy ran among the olive trees and hid, for well over a century. After heavy rains, old, gnarled fish were found in their branches, though the fishing nets stayed rolled. Still, wars and storms kept renewing themselves, forever young. It's gone on like that since they were first invented. Though in spring, young goats have trouble keeping up with their hooves." Angelos's beard had re-achieved a somewhat subdued bushiness in the rain, and swept him right back into the tavern. Nikos put his hands over his ears, and kept on running. But it was useless. "In Crete, you can't keep out stories with your hands," he heard Angelos warn, both from behind his left shoulder and inside his head. He detected, over the hiss of the rain, the chink of a glass of brandy in the voice.

A young male goat wandered over from Pavli's flock, and joined Nikos under the shelter of his tree. It had some folkdance pretensions, and did several leaps and side kicks, to gain his attention, only losing its footing once in the mud. It was curious about him. It moved its thick lips meditatively, chewing some grass, as if speaking. Nikos moved his lips in imitation. "No, you can't keep out stories, even with both hands," one of them said. Nikos wasn't sure which. Did it matter? The tone was surprisingly like Angelos's, whose tales could get anywhere. "When you're a born storyteller, Nikos, even a sharpshooting one, you can't keep stories away by hiding under an olive tree in the rain, even with a damned goat."

Nikos returned to the shed, accompanied by the damned goat. Odysseus Pappas behaved with new-found dignity, once given a name, wagging his short black beard as wisely as a priest. Nikos took out the air rifle, tacked up a fresh target, and began shooting. Odysseus curled up on the sacking in the shed and watched. The rain fell steadily, and Nikos shot away steadily in it. In half an hour, the sodden target was in tatters. Nikos peeled it off the door, and looked underneath. Washed by the rain, the embedded smooth-edged pellets shone as recently as his own. Odysseus shook one hoof, and wrinkled and moved his lips. "Kostas is still by far the best shot. He'll keep shooting for years yet. Like the sea, like storytellers, like spiders behind the old family portraits, sharpshooters always come back."

A Trip to the Fish Market

"They'll be bringing him home next Tuesday," the officer said. Then Dylan listened to the clop of military dress shoes depart down their driveway. The new tarmac gave back a clipped and well-polished sound. As though driveways, though deceptively hard and black, were really thin skins stretched and steam-rollered over deep underground and echoing cavities.

His mother tugged at her necklace as she began closing the door. Her mouth, as stretched as thin cotton thread, had been increasingly clutched at throughout the visit. His uncle was dead, killed by a roadside bomb in Afghanistan. When the officer broke the news, the room had gone as brilliantly black, for Dylan, as the buffed boot polish on the officer's shoes. Nevertheless, the officer's voice had continued, cautiously, in the darkness, as quiet and controlled as if he were trying, with hindsight, to defuse the bomb with his own adam's apple, before it went off. As the door closed, his mother's face snapped. Beads from the broken necklace pattered on the floor, rolling in every direction. He groped around, picking up beads and putting them carefully on the table. He picked up every one he could see, probably all that there were, but went on looking, not knowing, now, what he was looking for. He was looking for the sake of looking. But it didn't seem at all pointless.

The next morning, his mother stayed in bed with a migraine, waiting for the phone to ring from his father, away working the oil sands in Alberta. She called him into the bedroom, darkened by the cloudy scent that migraine suffering spreads as much as by the so-carefully adjusted drapes. She asked him to go down to the fish market for some cod for supper. Rumours were, there'd been a good catch. "Life must go on," she said, dropping coins into his palm as gingerly as if she didn't entirely believe what she said, and as though each coin throbbed with its own metallic and brightly burnished form of headache.

Outside, it was a relief to find the day throbbed only with sunshine. There were three hummingbirds at the sugary feeder on the magnolia tree. Usually they saw only one over the whole summer. Perhaps the profligate bush had just budded them as he stepped from the door, materializing hummingbirds out of his own unfounded hopes for seeing them, and not at all out of a long flight from lands to the south. They were wearing crimson balaclavas and tight-fitting lifejackets. They were too unexpected and numerous to be there, certainly too brightly coloured to be real. They went on sipping at the sugar feeder anyway. Then, in an eye-blink, they were gone, unable to achieve full existence.

The village fish market was down river, in the harbour. There'd been heavy rains over the last few days. The river was brown and seemed much higher mid-stream than at the banks, braiding and unbraiding its humped mane turbulently. A dented and rusty small bar fridge zipped past him, bobbing nonchalantly; then a large and partly submerged cardboard carton, with a cat sitting on it. The cat managed to leap off onto an over-hanging branch. It withdrew into the foliage, to recalculate its remaining lives very carefully.

The river was more argumentatively and implacably irreversible than it had ever before shown itself to be. The fridge was probably the one in his friend's, Jocko's, garage, full of cola and Jocko's Dad's beer. Wherever that fridge ended up by next Tuesday, it was clear the cola wouldn't get back to erupt in Jocko's magnificent thunderclap burp.—Even if his friend's cola-brown eyes still went on fizzing whenever they arm wrestled.

He thought of next Tuesday as like a black hole from which nothing could escape to reach today, either to better or worsen things. It was unable, even, to reach back and sway a single blade of grass, a single dandelion leaf, on the verge beside him. It was its own day, and would keep his uncle's homecoming guardedly to itself. There was no point in trying to think through, consistently, what it would be like. Though he sometimes found edges of images scattered about in his mind's eye, like sharp bits of glass, he couldn't make them fit together. Delighted to be home at last, his uncle would celebrate the homecoming by getting hitched to sweetheart Janey, with the vicar throwing handfuls of muddy earth down on the both of them, instead of confetti... It was impossible to see into the blackhole of next Tuesday past these confusing glitters at its edges.

The road led past several abandoned gardens and empty lots. There'd once been a number of nearby houses. They were all gone now, without a trace, gone wherever houses go to when they leave. He still wondered about that. Though one had burned down, and one had washed away, another had been hauled off on a truck. Presumably, it was its own new address.

The birds sang loudly as he walked. There was a virtuoso robin amongst them. It was as good as a barn dance fiddler playing a heel-kicking tune, one that can show up to the top of a girl's freckled legs. He wondered what its song was about. It seemed to lift to a space in the morning where a song can be, purely and simply, just about itself. Where the gap between a word and what it names disappears. Where people can return to us whenever we talk of them. Where we can straightforwardly give ourselves over to becoming something new, rather than just wording and rewording our New Year's resolutions. Something new but which has been there all along, like the song of the robin. At that point, he got a sharp pebble in a sneaker, and stopped listening to the birds.

The enclosed fish market was surrounded by pushy, loudmouthed evangelist gulls. They'd guided the boats back to harbour by chasing and dive-bombing them dutifully. Now they expected due payment. Fair's fair, right? "When's your poor uncle, our war-hero, coming home?" Several villagers asked him that. "Next Tuesday," Dylan replied. But the words felt awkward in his mouth. As though their meaning reached no further than he could spit at that moment—and he was pretty dry-mouthed and thirsty after his walk. There was an impassable distance between "coming home" and the black hole of next Tuesday. Uncle Josh was coming—by being entirely brought?

The sky was gathering greyness in oddly latticed clouds, like a fisherman's net about to haul in a fine catch of rain. In the darkling light, the potholed road just outside the main entrance to the market looked clogged with fish, not potholes—all heading for the unloading dock.

Indeed, it had been a good catch. Weaving swarms of fish were laid out on slopes of shaved ice. The bigger fish glinted with oily-looking rainbows, like a stretch of wet road with traces of gasoline on it. The scales of others seemed patterned and printed with columns of faint newsprint in no language he recognized. The prawns flickered with night lights at their tails. He tried to imagine the fish struggling as nets closed around them, their gasping for breath in the holds. But the fish were so freshly caught, they still looked alive. Except for their stillness, and perhaps an unblinking look of surprise in one or two of their eyes. If it had been a massacre in the deeps, it had been an entirely bloodless carnage.

"Dis haddock, she be so fresh, Missus Cobbler. If ye doan put her in yer oven as soon as youse home, she'll swim right outta your back door agin. Tak her head off afore you cook her, too. So fresh, she's still tinking her own toughts at de moment. Fish have deir own toughts, y'know."

"When's dat Uncle Josh comin' home, me boy?" the stall-holder asked. "Tuesday." His tongue slipped sideways in his mouth, as easily as an eel. Words and eel were out from under their rock. And the gap between words and next Tuesday was narrowing. Perhaps it just took practice. Only the gulls outside remained unsatisfied.

The Moving Business

I

In the moving and storage business, Josef Bartok is known as a man who notices things. It isn't just that he finds more clients than the rest of us one-van freelancers, spotting early signs that someone is thinking of beginning to think of a house move. Though he can read "Sofa for sale" cards nailed to a telegraph pole at a good hundred paces. Even after a hard day's work, when a group of us meet at the Toad and Egg, he stays strangely alert. He's almost vigilant, you might say. Yet there's something more to it than his being the first to see what any of us could've picked up on, like Tony's being given a dirty glass. He sits on the edge of his seat, eyes swivelling about, even when events drift by in a perfectly ordinary way. Sometimes, I've asked him who or what he's watching for, but he's only looked puzzled by the question, and answered, "Nothing in particular." Whatever this nothing is, it seldom leaves him alone. Wouldn't like my time taken up like that. Having Georgio as my brother is quite enough.

Last Friday, Josef seemed particularly vigilant in the bar. He shifted about on the bar stool, and kept crossing and uncrossing his legs. His jaws worked like heavy industrial clamps that kept missing their grip on something elusive, but obviously at the top of his work order. He left the room several times, saying "Won't be a minute, I've forgotten something." He wasn't heading for the washroom either. Eventually, I followed him, both out of curiosity, and to make sure he was alright. Once on the street, he let out his breath in an audible whoosh, like a whale surfacing and spouting hard. Then he walked about, jerking his head in all directions, like an agitated chicken. I got the odd sense that he hoped something was about to happen. After a bit, he calmed down, walked more slowly, and after strolling around the block, returned to his seat in the bar. I don't watch much TV, but he struck me as much like a reporter on an expensive assignment, anxiously looking for something, anything, to report on. I was more curious than ever. After all, he couldn't have been prospecting for clients on that block: it's full of big offices that our one-van operations can't handle.

I sat next to him, and asked, humorously, "Still watching out for that 'nothing in particular'?" He turned on me what were, for him, disturbingly untwitching and confiding eyes, and replied, "No, I'm quitting the business. Going into assembling pre-cut furniture. It's the obvious solution." Now, you've got to admit, what's clear to one man can be as thick as fudge to another. So I asked what he meant. The others were leaving, but I stayed behind as he began to tell me his story. Josef ran a one-man business, to our continued surprise, as he was slight enough to have been begotten by two closely stacked rakes. All the same, he sometimes managed even small pianos. What I'd never realized before was how furniture moving, for him, was mixed up with—well, I guess you could call it—a weird kind of sexy theology, if you'll excuse the expression. Yet how believable he made it seem. No wonder he was changing jobs. Moving pianos like that is too deep and confusing, quite apart from what happens if they drop on your foot.

II

Even as a toddler, Josef's mother had picked him out, in their large family, as "the boy with sharp eyes." He was far more curious than the rest. Only he and the dog ever knew what the dog was barking at, and the dog forgot more quickly. From the start, he could beat anyone at that memory game of listing what ten objects had been jumbled together on a now-covered tray. His mother had him play that game a lot, when her friends visited, as she lacked a matching tea set to impress them with instead. Perhaps as a result of this, he was soon able to enjoy almost any situation as a playful test in which he set himself to notice things around him.

When he started high school, his mother used to say that, with such sharp eyes, all sorts of doors would open for him in life, and he'd get any job he wanted. He remembered wondering about his mother's choice of words: surely it was windows and views that would offer things up to sharp eyes? But he did such wondering inwardly. His parents were strict, and they and questions made each other uncomfortable.

In his last few weeks of school, he returned to an activity he'd much enjoyed as a child. At weekends, he climbed the juddering ladder to the attic, to daydream a bit about where life might lead him, now. The attic had one small window of bevelled glass that looked out onto a raging sea of tilted garbage cans. On a sunny day, if he stood just right, the bevels filled the dusty attic with great curved rainbows of light. Even the two pigeons, which accompanied him on the eavestrough outside, drew on wondrous coats of many colours that they wore at no other time. He'd done some science at school, though his teacher, Mr. Phipps, told him he didn't attend to things long enough to do well at it. Still, he knew that the great robes of rainbow wrapped around him and the pigeons, were really there, guaranteed by temporary Mr. Phipps and the eternal laws of physics. Even the piles of pigeon droppings in the eaves-trough became as magnificent as a jeweller's window display. He thought, then, that this must be how one opened up the opportunities in life that his mother had spoken about. You cast your eyes about patiently, and found the right way to set them. Then you'd see what was really there, that other folk hadn't noticed.

Now, it's more relaxing than a massage, after a hard working week, to share childhood memories with a friend. And I've had lots of fun with prisms myself. But what had this got to do with Josef's jacking in his thriving business? I looked at my watch. That's when, with those eerily unblinking and untwitching eyes, he begged me to stay for just one more ale: "Sounds strange, but even an attic window can put you wrong for life, if you let it. Memories of it get stuck in your head like those long, sharp splinters that spear right through your work gloves." Isn't that worth staying to hear more about, especially when he's buying the round?

III

Josef was hired as an apprentice with a large moving company, right after school. His first job was to sort books in a doctor's house into similar sizes, before they were wrapped and packed in boxes. It's amazing how badly packed someone's books will end up, if you pack them in their order on the shelves. Clients hate that order being disturbed, of course. But if you keep to it, books of many different sizes slide past and into each other in a box, snapping each other's spines like badly trained wrestlers. The packers' order of the universe will put Proofs of the Existence of

God beside Spring Lingerie as part of the entirely proper sequence of things, if the books are the same size. Come to think of it, aren't beautiful women the best proof there can be that a God may exist?

Josef was left on his own to sort the books, after a brief explanation from the foreman. He worked at it conscientiously, and found he had a real knack for estimating book sizes accurately, at a quick glance, even if books were half hidden shyly behind each other. He enjoyed the true and concealed order of topics that sprang to his eye, as he sorted titles into piles. It was a wealthy doctor's house, and Fly Fishing belonged with Ritual Circumcision, in the secret order of knowledge he revealed to himself—a knowledge he was sure Mr. Phipps lacked.

He finished the job quickly, and the doctor's new young wife brought him tea as a reward. He was entirely inexperienced around women, but soon realized that, just as Jam Making belongs with Military Installations, so tea wasn't the only thing he was expected to stir to its full sweetness, reclining on the sofa. Like any teenager, he was amazed by the sensations that poured though his body like a previously undiscovered waterfall. But he was just as amazed to see, as he looked out from the midst of this waterfall, sharp-eyed as usual, that the world seemed to change around him—just as the attic did with its rainbows.

As he moved eagerly in love, he noticed the sun outside hop up and down beside him, keeping pace with his excitement. Tulips and dandelions joined in, in the flowerbeds beside the window, though perhaps the dandelions were the most vigorous. A cloud of brightly coloured butterflies drifted slowly across the garden, like the scent of a rose. The rainbows of their wings made him think of the rainbows in the attic. As he set his eyes right, they adjusted their fluttering to his own flight. He remembered watching them with a thrilled detachment, like an entomologist studying a hitherto unknown species so very hard that he was eventually able to join them. Out of the corner of his eye, he could see the sofa, too, hop cautiously in the general dance. He wished, humorously, it would hop towards the door, so that he and the foreman wouldn't have to carry it quite so far. When Josef and the doctor's wife lay quietly on the sofa afterwards, it seemed to him that the whole garden continued to levitate for a while. Though he wasn't sure why, she missed most of this. She mainly looked, bafflingly, inwards; or even kept her eyes, smilingly, closed.

Now Josef is no simpleton, then or now. He knew well enough that dandelions that jump are just an illusion, like the carpark spinning around you after a fairground ride on a landlocked wooden dolphin. But he was not prepared for what he noticed as they put their far flown clothes back on. The sofa, which was quite bulky, had moved at least a foot toward the door. That hop and skip had been real enough. Indeed, the foreman thanked him for making their job with the sofa that bit easier, though with no inkling of how joyously and unwittingly Josef had achieved it.

That night, Josef was over-tired and sleepless in bed. His first work experience, his first love experience, and his mother's interminable prayers over supper, all came together, in as surprisingly obvious an order as the titles of the books he'd sorted. He thought of how the psalms in the Bible speak of hills clapping their hands, of trees dancing. It suddenly struck him that King David must've written those songs out of how the world looked from the windows of his own kingly love-making; that David saw, with the eyes of love for Bathsheba, what loveless eyes can't imagine.

Josef got a tad serious—or was it just more sleepy?—and began to wonder how all the motion in the world had begun at the start of Everything Whatsoever. How had it got kick-started into the laws of motion that Mr. Phipps tested them on? That question had always intrigued him, though Phipps simply told him to get on with his homework. He began to wonder whether Everything had got kick-started—the atoms spinning, the planets whirling—propelled by an unabashed Love Force that had swelled the original Crotch of the universe with sheer aching desire. After all, his feelings with the doctor's wife had moved a sofa that he'd afterwards found he couldn't budge at all—and he'd surreptitiously pushed hard several times.

He remembers drifting off to sleep that night, proud and excited about his sexual awakening. Whether in a dream, awake, or that someplace between, he began to anticipate, hopefully, many more opportunities with girls coming his way. He began to dream of moving more sofas, even bigger bits of furniture, pianos maybe, if that wasn't too ambitious. Perhaps he could redeem, in his excitement with many, many, beautiful and gracious girls, the usual monotony of moving houses. Perhaps he could restore at least parts of the trade to that realm of sheer aching desire, from which it had been exiled into the drudgery of scraped paint, grazed elbows and bruised fingers. Then, like that Love Force, he'd be part, even if a small part, of the original Moving Business.

IV

After he'd served out his apprenticeship, Josef managed to set up on his own, with a buckled cube of rust on wheels that he restored into a small van. Clearly, the romantic opportunities of the Moving Business, even if near-galactic, were more available to a lone operator. Some days, he said, that van developed a finely tuned instinct, much better tuned than its engine ever was, for taking him to neighbourhoods where opportunities abounded. The steering wheel seemed to turn decisively on its own at crucial crossroads. It reminded him of his grandfather's horse, in stories his father told. His grandfather had been a doctor in the old country. After a long day of childbirths in isolated farmhouses on the steppes, grandfather would nod off in the sleigh. His mare would plod on, even through blizzards as white and sightless as cataracts, and carry him home, jingling its harness gently to awaken him when they arrived. Only twice did he wake up, in confusion, in a world he didn't recognize at all from an upturned sleigh, with huge crows—or was it black angels?—cawing and circling around him. That was when the mare visited stallions who'd called out to her. Though Josef never crashed his van, it did, on occasion, take him to some overturned worlds and encounters he couldn't begin to recognize. But it always got him back home from them, safely, afterwards.

Josef specialized in moving smaller pieces of furniture, sofas in particular—and beds, of course. The first time the headboard of a bed tapped on the wall in front of his startled eyes, vigorously and at enthusiastic length, like a biplane engine bursting into life, it struck him what a good flying machine he and his new friend made. It was as though they had wings at their shoulders and feet. Afterwards, the bed had definitely taxied closer to the landing. Later, he learned to align a bed's casters beforehand, and to remove the chocks of carpets and slippers. As he came into his physical prime, he moved several small pianos single-handedly. That was harder in the Moving Business. But making love under a piano has its own delights, he assured me. If the piano has good wood grain to it, looking up into it is like looking up into the tracery of branches and leaves in a forest. That was the closest he got to a forest most years, as jobs in town kept him busy.

Of course, there were bad days, when the most the Moving Business could manage to shift was a vase or two along a mantlepiece. That was quite pointless, as it's easy enough just to pick them up, anyway—though the big brass ones can sometimes unbalance you with their weight. Now and again, a vase would fall and smash. He'd hear it hit the ground, but be unable, *in flagrante,* even to roll out of the way of the fragments. It seemed strange to him that those were often the days when he pleased his ladies the most. The smashed vases didn't bother them at all. But it left him unsatisfied, professionally, as a mover. He'd obviously been careless, and forgotten that necessary glance from the corner of his eye, while love-making, at what furniture needed moving. That was the apparently so necessary double-mindfulness, that spontaneously aligned the motions of love with where things needed to go.

He'd worked for ten years like this, remaining a bachelor—as the Moving Business required of him. Then, last month, by chance, his van had taken him to an address where he recognized his client as that doctor's wife who'd first opened vistas of a profession before him. She recognized him straightaway, too, with a smile that made him unexpectedly nervous, since it was as soft as down that tickled his face, with no pushy quill of hard come-on behind it. Such a smile, from attractive clients, was beyond his range of experience. At first, he wondered whether his van was pursuing some deeply concealed needs of its own, as he'd never revisited clients.

His uncomfortableness soon disappeared, however, as she quietly pointed out what furniture needed moving, sometimes putting a hand on his shoulder, very gently. When he'd carried out the furniture, she brought him tea, and they fell to talking. She was now divorced, and had seen some life. Well, to shorten the story, they ended up in the very bed which he noted, with a dawning sense of irony, she'd said was the one that didn't need moving.

He'd been back several times, entirely not to move that bed, and something was happening that was different, for him. If the sun hopped and skipped outside, it was now doing it on its own, and he didn't notice. He got more and more lost, and then found, and then lost again, with her, and experienced little else. Just once, he'd tried to recall himself to his old dual consciousness, with great effort, like a man struggling to carry a giant, cast-iron chandelier on one shoulder. But he managed it only long enough to notice the parrot cage on its stand beside them. As he glimpsed it out of the corner of his eye, it began to tilt and slide past them on the wooden floor. The parrot squawked in alarm and shouted "Pleased t'meet ya!" several times, in a decidedly unpleased voice. He looked away quickly, and fell back, deeply and endlessly, into Francesca. Afterwards, he was hugely relieved that the cage seemed pretty much in its original place. Though the parrot had taken a vow of glum silence, and pecked at its mirror like a crazed assassin.

V

"I've mulled it over for days," Josef said. "Finally made up my mind to change careers, walking around the block just now." Something had shifted in him. Life was no longer, and constantly, a bevelled window he had to press eyes to, with a thrilled detachment, to make things be what they, so magnificently, could. "It's a new thing for me: my eyes can close in Francesca's arms, and I even fall asleep." He walked out of the bar looking more relaxed than I'd seen him for a long while. Josef looked, if I may steal one of his expressions, like a man who's just had a large cast-iron chandelier lifted clean off his shoulders into the truck.

So that's how my friend decided he couldn't go on with his very successful business. If gods or other men want to redeem furniture moving from its workaday monotony to sheer aching desire, he'll be leaving it to them from now on, thanks very much. And if the gods can fall head over heels for each other, perhaps even they'll quit their Moving Business, leaving atoms to whirl about quite comfortably on their own.

Beyond Words

The first real snow of winter is falling outside the Adam's living room window. It's Friday, late afternoon. The young couple isn't back from work yet. Though the apartment is empty, it seems deliberately quiet, with expectation. No one's there to look out of the window, which is a good time to see things.

On the construction-site opposite, three workmen are bundled in parkas, their hoods up. They have blonde beards and moustaches. They're kneeling on top of the scaffolding, inspecting a length of duct. Fluffy snow settles on them quickly. The workmen begin to look like white-robed Russian pilgrims, crawling on their knees, in penance, to some holy site in the steppes. But when more snow falls on the men and their beards, they look as much like huge larval butterflies, suspended above the street, about to hatch out of their white cocoons, though still deliberating over what to emerge as. The window glitters uncertainly in stray rays of light from the already setting sun.

A young woman walks through the churchyard beside the construction site. She's just come from the deserted church. She'd switched off both her cellphone and disc player in the main aisle, though leaving the earphones in place. She'd stood there briefly but intently, and formed a few words in her head, very careful not to move her lips by the shadow of a tremor of a whispered, sibilant hiss. She didn't want even an empty church to jump to the conclusion that she was praying, when she, herself, couldn't have said. What she did know was that she had a frustrated need to clear up a misunderstanding with the obstacles and delays of the universe. Perhaps it was like the very beginnings of road rage, but much less focused. "May we please, please, get me pregnant and have a child. I'm thirty-five already. How much longer do we have to wait?"

The sun had answered immediately, bursting in on the polish-reeking brass plates and candlesticks. All the same, the request followed her out into the snow, its lips still moving quietly in her head, worried that it had, yet again, not been heard properly. It repeated itself carefully among the pure and unstained ikons of the gathering icicles.

Snow is drifting amongst the tombstones as she walks the path between them. The drifts shift in the changing wind. Tombstones bob up and down amongst them, as though being waved encouragingly, perhaps by great-great-grandfathers who want to hitch a ride with her, in her energetically red, high-heeled shoes, to get out of the implacable inactivity of the graveyard as quickly as possible.

The woman crosses the road in front of the scaffolding. The three workmen turn and watch her, their thoughts very straight-backed with arms akimbo. Whatever forgiveness they were looking for in the duct, they have found, instead, in her swaying walk. The air seems filled with a mercy of sparks all around her. Their eyes do the welding. A few moments later, the key turns in the door to the apartment. Naomi is home.

Naomi puts on a fragrant silk house-coat, as yellow as tulips, and stands by the window for a moment, watching the snow. The three huge cocoons on the scaffolding opposite look up with coy lust, pretending, among themselves, to be watching the weather. She moves nimbly around the room on arched bare feet, each toe alert in a different colour of nail varnish. As her wise grandmother had told Naomi, when showing her how to paint her toes as a little girl, "If this makes you happy, just be happy, don't ask why."

Naomi tidies things: a copper plate straightened on the wall, cushions puffed up on the sofa. Then she goes to the kitchen, and wraps herself in a large, old apron. The apron has so many pockets, and pockets inside of and on top of pockets, that she looks, for a moment, like a blizzard of pockets with a person attached as a mere afterthought. But it's soon clear who's in charge. She skips around the kitchen, gathering garlic cloves and spice jars from different cupboards. She drops them into the pockets of her apron, then goes to the pan on the stove.

"So, my Grandmother's apron, you've come a long way, from Cyprus to Canada, to help me make another supper. My Grandmother, that famous matchmaker! Who collected names of lonely hearts, across far flung villages, in her many pockets. She who could pull out and match names with such amazing success. When your name got tucked into one of her pockets, she sure knew all your secrets, with her sharp eyes and those awkward questions. And if she didn't pull the perfect groom out of a pocket, it would at least be a much-needed ointment for skin-rash. Well, dear Grandmother, I'm no matchmaker, but help me match up a perfect seasoning for our soup from your pockets."

Naomi stops talking, and stands tightly enfolded in both silence and her apron in front of the stove. She doesn't look at a recipe book or list. Her hands move as quickly as a jazz pianist's, practiced yet improvisatory in their sureness. Out of her scattered pockets and into the soup pot, lickety-split, go cardamom, cumin, coriander, turmeric, cinnamon, cloves, ginger, black peppercorn and mace. Some stock splashes up onto her face, and settles there unnoticed, like an attractive caramel freckle.

"I wonder what the bestselling spice mix of the year will be? If I could discover it now, I'd make a million for Grandma's old apron and me." Truth to tell, Naomi's thoughts are on trying to make a baby after this very supper. That's the blending that's really on her mind. But she can't say it out loud, even to herself. It would tempt fate far too sorely. As her Grandmother taught her long ago, even the most carefully coloured toes won't keep fate away. Instead, she smiles hopefully at her feet. As if to increase her chances, but maybe only because the stove is making the room too warm, she goes to the window and opens it slightly. A breeze comes in with that sherbet-cold taste of first snow, and adds to the aroma of simmering soup. The kitchen suddenly gets bigger, making a much larger savour, linked, through the evening sky, to the minerals of mountain slopes and the far salts of seas. Might this be the spice mix of the twenty-first century? With the evening meal cooking, Naomi sits on the sofa, looking out the window, waiting for Jon to come home. Snow piles up on surrounding rooftops. At first cautiously, and then more ambitiously, it cantilevers out in white overhangs, linking eavestrough to eavestrough, arching away everywhere, across the whole city, uniting one house to another as parts of a single ice palace. By the same movement, it merges one family's muffled dreams and disasters indiscernibly into another's, as parts of the same gathering silence. She wonders whether, when people get home from work, and hang up their dripping parkas, it isn't mostly the same dreams and disasters in the back of everyone's closet, whatever the address is.

As Naomi and Jon eat supper, she grows more apprehensive with each mouthful, remembering their wedding of ten years ago. "Your brothers and cousins all either had beards like you, or five-o'clock shadows, more like going on six. My cheeks got nettle rash from greeting those bristles and whiskers. I had to keep powdering in the restroom. They stood around us, staring at me, virtually out of a broad-shouldered hedge of wiry black hair. I'm sure they were thinking, she's so skinny and pale and flatchested, she'll never have children. And them so massive from farm work, even their eyes rippled with biceps."

Jon, in the flickering remnant of an argumentative mood from the office, disagrees. "But they know darned well that some of their skinniest cattle are the ones that calve and milk best. Anyway, since when did you turn into a she-goat?" Then the flicker is snuffed out in laughter. He puts a hand lightly on her shoulder, stroking it gently. It's the only relevant answer.

Naomi raises her shoulder to his fingers, as warm and soft as a milksnake in the sun. Her body speaks back to him in its own braille language, as it always has done, since that first day he plucked up courage to brush against her, as lightly as a flustered butterfly. She adds, "My friend Marcie told me, at work, that God couldn't be everywhere. So He created mothers. Well, there's so much going on in the world today, He still can't be everywhere, can He? I'd be happy to help out—here's a willing recruit." Before the words are spoken, she knows, self-consciously, that they're merely nervously redundant. The milksnake had said "Here I am" far more effectively.

Just then, the phone rings. It's a three-way call they've arranged with both of their mothers, to celebrate the beginning of the long weekend. Three-way calls were Naomi's idea for keeping them all in touch, across the country. Jon found the calls awkward at first, as Naomi's mother speaks only Greek, while his mother speaks only Czechoslovakian. But Jon quickly discovered that Naomi is a practitioner not just of simultaneous, but of magical, translation. Words change languages in mid-air around her, hardly having time to rattle her eardrums. Whole cultures and dress outfits change in mid-sentence, mid-grammatical construction, mid-syllable even: a jacket into a shawl, a church into a mosque, a circle dance into a new husband into a Viennese waltz.

For Jon, the effortless spontaneity of Naomi's translations, always delivered in lilts of laughter, adds something indefinable to what any of them had originally said. It's as though they complete each other's sentences by metamorphosing snugly into each other's lives. Knowing their mothers' eager hopes for them, he, too, has sometimes come close to expecting, during the phone calls, to become a grandmother himself, even if to his own child: "but as soon as possible, by sometime next year; and don't forget to phone me when you're sure!"

The call with their mothers went well. Jon feels relaxed and happy. All that could be magically translated, has been said. When he hangs up, he cradles language, itself, back into its ever-ready receiver, for now. All he can manage to say to Naomi is, "Let's go to bed." His voice sounds strangely guttural in his ears. As though Naomi is instantly translating it into yet another language, as he speaks. Or as though she's now empowered, by his voice box, to speak for both of them, unanimously. In this matter, he certainly doesn't disagree with herself.

They tumble onto the bed in a free-fall of wordless laughter. Naomi, as usual, matter-of-factly turns her grandmother's old ikon of the Annunciation to face the wall, on her bedside table.

Jon catches only a quick glimpse of the Archangel Gabriel's leaping approach, sandals barely touching the ground, hand outstretched in welcome, blue robe taut with speed, wings upraised, in an odd medieval perspective, like the stilled rotor blades of a taxiing helicopter. Jon doesn't share Naomi's concern about ikons peeking at lovemaking. He notices, with surprise, that it's a sensitivity that runs deep, as, this time, she covers the ikon with the old apron too, just to make sure. He almost says something, but Naomi, in his voice box, has decided, for both of them, that there's nothing more to be said.

In the middle of the night, Jon sits up quietly in bed, so as not to disturb Naomi. Through the open bedroom door, he can see it's still snowing outside the big living room window. A gusty wind can't make up its mind which direction to sneeze in. Snowflakes dart backwards and forwards, circling vertically, rather than drifting to the street. He notices, with surprise, that they're reddish in the street-light, as though they have their own strange flesh and blood, hitherto unsuspected by humankind.

Jon has woken up into an impressionable mood that seems, to him, more awake than just being awake, though he knows his practical wife would think him still half asleep and merely dozy. So why wake up Naomi, just to be unable to share things with her? As he looks over to her side of the bed, he can make out, in the gloom, the apron she's put over the icon. It's humped and creased, and seems to be standing almost upright on its own, about to achieve its first steps as an unworn apron, an unchallenged first for the Guinness book of records. Many of its pockets yawn invitingly wide open among the folds.

He wrinkles his nose with pleasure, wondering what they may blend into being from the savour of their warm bodies in the bed. Then he wonders, but only for a passing moment, whether such fancies are at all appropriate for the no-nonsense bank cashier he's supposed to be. This second wonder is easily supplanted by a sound suspiciously like Gabriel's rotor blades, whirring ceaselessly behind the match-making apron; though it might have been the refrigerator's motor. He goes to the refrigerator for a drink of iced water. On his careful stumble back to bed, he knocks a book off Naomi's bedside table. But it's not on the agenda of his more-than-awake and grandly synthesizing mood to notice the merely mundanely out-of-place.

The glowing snowflakes darting about outside now strike him as like a vigorous storm of pollen, even eager human seed, flying through the darkness. Naomi had said that this weekend was calculated to be the height of her receptivity. It takes only a single sperm. Immediately, he can feel that single sperm, deep inside him, a little tadpole at the ready, hidden in the blizzard and sheer white-out of his thighs, relentlessly transmitting its singular and unique rapture to him, for its hoped-for but unknowable destiny. He becomes unsure whether it's an about-to-be-conceived first-born, or the first snowfall, he's experiencing, or perhaps both.

His mind races on. He puts off a decision on what to feel for all the unlucky tadpoles, that vast majority who have no vote in a matter where no democracy, sadly, prevails. Perhaps they become the dust motes you can see in a room on a sunny day, floating in mid-air in an insubstantial sub-existence, each one of them, equally, the eldest never-to-be-begotten child. The imponderable numbers, the sheer mathematics of it, draws him on. He begins to snore.

Naomi wakes up promptly, just before dawn. The snow has stopped. There's now a light hail. It makes a sound like cackling hens laying particularly well on the siding of the house. Outside the living room window, drifts lie everywhere, in long curves, like huge white eggs, having no beginning and no end under the rising sun. She looks at Jon. He's sleeping, doubled up and wrapped only in the wide wooly blanket of his beard.

Before stirring him, she picks up her apron, and quickly turns the ikon around to face the room again. She always hopes Jon hasn't really noticed her lingering superstitions. It isn't something she knows how to talk about. The sudden half light wakes up the ikon, as she's noticed dawn can do to pictures. She catches a glimpse of Gabriel's toes uncurling in his sandals, his legs stretching under his tautened blue robe. Mary is still hidden in the shadow of a canopy in some fourteenth century church in Macedonia—where the original of this copy was prayed into paint.

Naomi is startled to hear the fluttering sound of wings in the room. She kneels and crosses herself. Truth to tell, this has happened to her before. Embarrassed, she turns her movement smoothly into an effort to retrieve her slippers from under the bed. She spots two pigeons outside on the ledge. Their wings unfurl like sails. An unbelievable scent fills the room, like incense. She tries to puzzle it out, as she puts on her apron. It could be mace, cumin and freshly ground ginger, with perhaps a touch of motor-oil through the slightly open window. She makes a mental note of it. She can't remember ever using that combination before. Perhaps she accidentally spilt some spices on the floor, yesterday evening. She'll try it out, now, for breakfast.

Naomi reaches out with a corner of her apron, to brush some dust from the glass front of the ikon. There's what looks like a light beading of perspiration on the Archangel's face, something she'd not noticed before. Could it be her own? After all, it had been a warm and active night. But it won't wipe off, is condensation under the glass. "Getting a sweat on, then, announcing fulfillments all night, all over the town? Hard work being an Archangel!" She laughs softly, then catches sight of her day-book on the floor. Jon is waking up. "Jon did you stumble about in the night?" His head is still filled with sitting up quietly in bed, entranced by the vast swarming of human seed in the storm. "Don't think so" he says, lips pursed for a shave, but also to hold in his thoughts, realizing it could well come out wrong, at this early hour, at any hour, and sound obscene to Naomi, if he says a single word more. Jon strokes her shoulder gently as he passes her. Around the world, grass-snakes in the sun simply stir warmly.

Naomi has the odd picture slide into her mind of her day-book being accidentally knocked to the floor by the heel of a sandal that was carefully rotating itself back into the ikon's interior. As her matchmaking grandmother from Paphos would have told her: this is something else that can happily stay beyond words in their marriage. She skips to the kitchen, and, in expectant silence, gathers jars of spices in her pockets, moving to the counter to scatter them prodigiously into a bowl of fresh fruit salad.

A Conspiracy of Grandmothers

When Dante wrote his *Inferno*, he had not been delayed at London's Gatwick Airport. Something comes over a building when large numbers of people are kept waiting in it long past the furthest ends of their wits. The building starts some large-scale tomfoolery, or goes off on a holiday of its own. An airport terminal can think up all sorts of architectural features its planners never intended. The lounge where you left a wife and small baby will deliberately relocate itself, as you try to find your way back with a plate of shriveled sandwiches. While lounges trade places, corridors heave themselves up on a slant, making sure they are uphill whichever way you walk. Carpets show their true feelings, and drag themselves against your feet, with all the animosity of cornered hedgehogs realigning their bristles.

Buildings get the most out of hand when you are travelling anxiously with a tired young wife and a three-week old baby. Terminals seem to have an ancient grudge against infants. Whatever babies once did to them is not something that can be forgiven. The full weight of scheming is thrown against these swaddled offenders. It's not something any young father has much hope of handling. At least, that's how it struck me, as I waited with my small new family at Gatwick Airport, in a mislaid lounge of an overdue terminal, for a long-delayed flight to Canada.

As the day dithered by, the lounges filled up with people. Garbled voices over the loudspeaker said the delay was caused by a combination of industrial disputes in starboard engines, mechanical failure by the rain, and an unseasonably heavy downpour of baggage handlers. It made as much sense as everything else. As untaken seats became scarcer, travelers organized themselves into protective groupings. Duty-free bags of scarves and perfume were co-opted as boundary-markers. Neighbouring encampments tried to keep each other and the surrounding limbo at bay. Tents and whole villages of newspapers sprang up. Drinking establishments were founded among the largest suitcases. But it soon became clear that a three-week old baby was too much of a newcomer to be admitted into such well-established tribes.

At first, our son slept, waking only to drink another of the feeding bottles of milk we had brought with us. Then the bottles ran out. At this point, he showed himself totally unswayed by such vain imaginings as international date lines and difficulties with jet engines. He knew only that the entire planet was suddenly bitten through with hunger right under his own skin. With an understanding of Biblical traditions uncanny in one so young, he promptly began lamentations for the end of all history. I had to admire his unabashed stand.

There was nowhere quiet we could take him, to think through the problem. The ladies' washroom behind us had already proved to be foggy with girls from Liverpool, organizing a dance. The closest corridor had been given over to an exhibition game of bowls, involving empty beer bottles and someone's uncle's gargantuan sock rolled up as a ball. In 1969, that just about exhausted the possibilities. Besides, routes through the surrounding encampments had been sealed off by a rapid proliferation of duty-free boundary-markers. It would take patient diplomacy to get us through. And patience is not something a prophet, berating the world in its eleventh hour, can tolerate.

With no alternative in the overcrowded terminal, my wife resorted to a practice carefully prepared for by several million years of evolution, which evidently had foreseen such problems in international airports. She began to breastfeed our son under her cape. This practice had not been seen before among our neighbours, for it immediately produced a series of loud clicking noises among them. It was as if they were carrying geiger counters in their hand-baggage, and we had released a level of activity that was lethal to them. Anyway, the clicking spread rapidly across the lounge. My son seemed right in predicting some large scale catastrophe.

Our prospects of dealing peacefully with our fellow travellers were declining alarmingly when, out of nowhere, seven very elderly ladies, dressed all in black with bags of knitting, suddenly surrounded us. They came out of perfectly thin air, which I'd thought existed only in my father's elaborate stories. They had eyes only for our son, smiling beatifically as though he were every grandson they ever had waited for. You would have sworn they had just stepped off a fishing smack from the island of Crete or Santorini. They carried that indefinable smell of the sea with them, and walked with the sea legs of perpetual sailors.

I can't remember them uttering a word. But, without their needing to speak in some language I would probably only misunderstand perfectly, I knew why they had come. They had just walked up the cobblestones from a little harbour below, where the sea was still throwing its waves about, beyond the white harbour wall. They had come to greet our new son's arrival, and to help organize either his christening or his immediate ritual circumcision, whichever most mattered to them; and one of them certainly did.

The grandmother who stopped opposite me particularly sticks in my mind. As I knelt by my wife, offering a young father's ineffectual well meant advice, I first noticed the old lady's small black shoes, scuffed but carefully polished. Both soles were worn steeply, on the left side. Wherever she went, she took with her the secure sense of whatever steep hill she still habitually worked on. Apparently she always faced in the same direction, as she moved backwards and forwards along rows of vines or cabbages, looking out at the far horizon from where the strong winds of life come. Now, with her years and calm, she could anticipate those winds before they arrived, and knew how to help others wait for and stand in them. As proof, her grey hair had a well developed and wiry will of its own, and leant out from her forehead as though it had just struck a bargain with several squalls.

As she watched my wife and son, she kept raising both hands in a gesture of delighted encouragement. She clutched one hand in the other, and lifted it, palm outward and open, like a tired bird being helped on a journey it was still very eager to make. Each time she did so, I was caught up in the swirling scents of camphor and candle wax. Though her coat was frayed at the cuffs, it was clearly her best, and got unfolded from the warm darkness of a camphorwood chest only for such occasions as this. The smell of camphor affected me as incense sometimes does. I lost all sense of place. I could've sworn the lounge filled with a gusting breeze; and I thought I could hear the fish-heavy tide coming in at last, with a silvery rush, up the puddled and patiently waiting runway.

I looked up at her face, trying to hold onto something. The passing years had screwed it up like a piece of brown paper. But she had carefully uncrumpled it, smoothing it out the best she could, to be used again and again, together with wool from old sweaters. The many lines on her face somehow let through a warming light. It was like looking at a frail parchment, illuminated from behind in a museum. Her face recorded the lessons of a lifetime, what she now stood for: the hungry must be fed, infants and the weak protected, and the proud condemned to the discomfort and clicking of their own lives.

The grandmothers formed a protective circle around us, still not speaking, except with their smiles. My son sucked on, uninterruptedly and with determination. Beneath their encouraging gaze, he proceeded to salvage the entire planet, turned the danger of its eleventh hour aside, and then promptly fell asleep at the nipple. This, too, was what they had been waiting for; and they were overjoyed not to have missed it. That one so small should achieve so much clearly impressed them. Looking back, my wife and I agreed that it was at that moment, though quite separately, that we decided to call him David.

I took my son and his new name from my wife, and wrapped them both up in the white shawl that my mother had given us only that morning. It was to remind us to journey back one day to visit her, bringing a tall young man to talk away the clouds with her. I rocked my son and his name in my arms. When I looked up again, meaning to smile back my thanks to the seven old ladies, they had gone without a trace, vanished in a matter of seconds. They'd left nothing behind to show they'd ever been there: not a mislaid ball of wool, not even a single dried fig. I felt a growing respect for my father's stories. I had always loved them. Now I knew his lies could be perfectly true. It was then that I realized not a click could be heard all over the lounge. And the disorienting tomfoolery of the building had stopped. Once again, it was just there to serve us. Not long afterwards, our flight was announced, and we came to Canada.

Our son David is now seventeen. Often, over the years, I have thought back to that incident at the airport. It was one of those accidental meetings, barely a meeting even, that makes life far more of an adventure than anything you can plan. I had supposed that, by now, those ladies would no longer be among us. They seemed ancient at the time, and as dry as biscuits. Recently, I've had to revise that opinion.

My new job involves a fair bit of travelling, and I'm often killing time at airports and bus terminals. On several occasions, and in various parts of the world, I'm sure I've caught glimpses of those same old ladies. Each time, they've been smiling beatifically, either at a very small baby, or at someone who was unwell. Once, at the airport in Singapore, they were joined by an eighth lady of Oriental rather than Mediterranean aspect. They seemed to know each other already, too well to need to speak in greeting.

They all seem to belong to a reasonably well funded worldwide organization. I asked two old aunts of mine about it. They're both in their nineties. They didn't look surprised, but wouldn't answer questions. It took some while to dawn on me that they were probably members themselves. There's something odd, but good, going on in the world; and we ought to know more about it. I've tried to talk to David about this. But he only laughs, and says he's too tall now for me to go on telling him stories. My wife says not to worry, he'll find out soon enough. He's got a sharp eye for girls already, and is looking forward to doing some travelling of his own.

A Cobbler

The small shed at the bottom of the garden had been off limits to the boy during the first day of his visit to his grandparents. But, today, with heavy weather scowling in under dark brows from the sea, grandfather O'Connor took Patrick by the hand after breakfast, and led him down the yard. "You wonder what I do in there? Well, come and see. It's not a day to walk the beach again, unless you'd like to be a lot wetter than water. But you're not cut out to be another rock-pool, are you?"

Close up, the shed revealed itself as built largely from the paradox of insecurely cemented old and chipped bricks held together by a sheer and secure wall of solid ivy. Grandfather unlocked the door, turned around, and walked in backwards. "Why do that, grandpa?" "Well, now, work fits better into life when you arrive as if you were leaving, and leave as if you were arriving."

Inside, on a work-bench, the boy noticed some old shoes, thread, and a small hammer. "My mother was a sailor—cook on a steamer—and father made dresses. Though they probably met after she'd become a virgin—and I hope you're old enough to know about that—they were always very happy. I decided to be a cobbler, just to round things out." Grandfather put a tack between each finger of his left hand, then, rather awkwardly, picked up a well-worn open Bible and the hammer with his right. "I always do this at the start of work. If, in the beginning there was a word, after that there was a hammer." Hammer and Bible rose and fell, as he gave a single tap at a shoe. Patrick was uncertain, for a moment, whether grandpa was hammering with the Bible, and his lips moving silently as he somehow read from the hammer. "Beautiful psalm, that." He laid the Bible down on a vise. "First, I'll resole these old shoes." The tapping increased to a blur of sound. Patrick slid onto a stool and watched.

Rain began on the tin roof. It, too, increased to a blur of sound. Grandfather and the clouds overhead kept time with each other, a knock for each metallic, pinging drop. The storm was clearly of the most industrious sort. Patrick felt warm and comfortable on the stool. He drowsed trustfully, as busy rain took over cobbling the shoes, and grandpa O'Connor omnipresently filled with fresh water all the cattle troughs in the fields. He was awoken by grandma bringing out a tin mug of tea for each of them, and two large sugar-lumps for grandpa.

"Here you are, me boyos." A scent of flowery perfume and salted onions leaped from her like a wild cat, not at all perfume of the gently wafting sort. There was a small patch of dried saliva around her lower lip. She'd been stirring soup and tasting it to get it just right. The saliva around her tight straight lips made her mouth look like one of the lace-bordered lavender-scented sachets that Patrick's maiden aunts kept among their clothes in a drawer. Grandma left again, as quietly as any sachet.

Grandpa gripped a sugar lump between the awls of his pointed teeth and sucked tea through it slowly. The sugar lump got smaller, and grandpa's mouth wrinkled more and more tightly around it. He worked on, between sips, sewing up a pitch-forked hole in the side of a work boot, until it pursed with self denial and disappeared. Then he took the other large sugar lump between his teeth, and began to stitch up another gaping side of a boot. Patrick sipped too, and thought of his height marked on the wall of the kitchen, yesterday, by grandma. She'd said he'd only get bigger, and very much so. He was grateful to be an exception to the apparently cosmic process of big into disappearingly small that grandpa was working with now.

"Do you know, now, me boy, what those rascals are, on the top shelf?" He pointed at what looked like a row of solid wooden shoes. They were of different sizes, in different woods, but lined up neatly, like the feet of a forest of soldiers planted on parade. Though there was dust on other shelves, these shoes all gleamed brightly. Grandfather flicked a cloth across them, like a sergeant-major checking that all passed inspection satisfactorily.

"They're called 'lasts.' They're the shapes on which I can lay out me leather and stitch up shoes for just about everyone in the village. Whatever folks do when they wear me shoes, I've already sewn and nailed into place that they can do it. Tap-tap: each long work day, quick dance step, stumble, flying fall, marriage procession down the aisle. Also, that alternative heavy breathing meet up, toe-to-toe, behind the nearest dark hedge. —And I hope you're old enough to know about that. It's all taken care of in this little workshop. Quite a responsibility, I can tell you."

Grandfather O'Connor was a tall man. To not overpower customers by his height, he'd learned to be assertively innocuous, by deliberately pitching his voice so it seemed to issue softly from his abdomen. He loved telling stories. As he spoke of his responsibility as creator of the futures of all the feet he shod, his voice shook with an hypnotic quality. As though the tale were telling itself, and had to be told whether or not anyone were there to listen to it. As though it were shaping his lips around it, rather than being shaped by them. His eyes widened, not looking at Patrick at all, not focused on anything around them, but looking at landscapes and lives a long way off, though somehow also in the middle of the room.

"Be Jayzus, this leather is tough." O'Connor's teeth gripped tightly as he hauled the thread through and back and through. Patrick noticed that when grandfather gritted his teeth together for a while, whether while sewing, or, in the evening, around his belching black factory of a pipe, wrinkles appeared at the corners of his mouth. They were deep, and began to look functional, like gills on a strange fish. But O'Connor was no mackerel floundering out of water. Though hauling hard at the thread, he hummed contentedly. Patrick looked quickly around the room, trying to catch a suggestion of the natural but invisible element that his grandfather had evolved to swim in.

As the morning passed, a pile of newly repaired shoes mounted up on the table. Grandfather O'Connor was quietly absorbed in his work for a while. Patrick looked out of the one small window, that some gull had used as an action painter's palette. Rain still fell. A low, grey, oblong cloud drifted up that looked like a badly varnished half open door. A kestrel peeled down from it, as though it had successfully got through. Patrick looked across the bay to the horizon. With the incoming tide, the morning's quota of waves was piling up on the rocks. Waves grazed, tore, and wore themselves thin on the rocks, but then retreated, repaired themselves, and marched in again, sometimes strolling nonchalantly, and successfully leaped over the low headland.

Deliberately half-closing his eyes, Patrick had a sense of the long-enduring sea molding all the mounting changes among the waves: sudden high-heeled stilettos and spikes of spray, sandal-loose ripples slipping loosely from side to side in the rock pools, crashing steel-capped work boots of surf kicking hard along the cliffs. He wondered whether there was some kind of ageless sea-last, bigger by far than the shoe lasts on the shelf: water as deep and dark and smooth and featureless as mahogany, responsible for, and underlying, all storms.

After a quick lunch back at the house, Patrick took a walk in the garden. The rain, open-mindedly, was considering the pros and cons of turning into mist instead. A crop of puddles across the lawn nearly outnumbered the dandelions. The now gentle breeze plaited grey reflections in the puddles: more plaits than there were ruffles on the collar of grandma's sheep-smelling sweater. Patrick walked up to the fence around the garden, and leaned on a post, looking at the start of the pine forest not far away. The post swayed as unsteadily as a first-year boy after a rugby scrum. Other posts down the line staggered sickeningly too, and a section of fence crashed to its knees. Alarmed, and with the stalwart rain deciding to stay as rain, Patrick ran back to the shed. "Grandpa, why are the fence posts all so loose?" Why such poor fencing, when grandpa repaired and made shoes so patiently and well?

"Lookie, me boy, the answer to that is another question. Did you walk into the shed backwards or not?" Patrick was confused by the striking irrelevance of the question. Yet the confusion somehow cleared his mind in a focusing way. That often happened to him with his grandfather. He was put on a wide-eyed alert to catch the drift, or whether there was one at all. "Go on, out you step, and come in backwards. Make it quick, now. The fence posts won't wait." Patrick complied, in rain more determinedly stalwart than ever. "Good, now I'll learn you how work, even at putting in very shallow fence posts, fits well into life. And you can try walking into the cinema backwards, too. They might think you was coming out, and not charge you at all."

"See, each time the fence tumbles, I put it back a bit further out. But I put it in real shallow, so it's soon ready to trip and fall again. If it's being stiff-necked and steady, I can always give a little push. Then up it goes again, a bit further out once more. There's a real art to it, at the highest level, and not so easily learned. Who says, as you add more years, you shouldn't gain more land? I'd like my back gate to end up right against the forest, in a year or two. A way out straight onto the mysteries of dark shade and birdsong and plenty of berries. Not much time. I'm eighty-three already."

O'Connor's voice softened, and seemed to come straight from his navel. He no longer looked at Patrick, but, perhaps, at dark branches in the very middle of the room. He caught his breath, stretching his jaw. The gills at either side of his mouth appeared, and opened and closed with calm efficiency. "So what's so surprising to you, me boy? Don't you gotta keep changing your own boundaries, all over your life? Some young men get married in a rush that surprises the Sunday-best troussies right off them—and you're of an age to know this, are you not? Others plan to, but then stay closer in, stuck to their dear old Irish mothers. Some go with girls almost before they start school, but then walk across the threshold of one of the darkest of forests—into those long, wind-whistling aisles of the priesthood. Though we know we're so often at thresholds, we forget the gateposts keep moving."

Grandfather O'Connor lifted down one of the lasts, and put it on the work-bench. "Don't use this one often. It's for a light dance-shoe that'd fit the feet of most of the O' Flaherty men in the village. But only one of them has ever jigged much—my old friend Sean. Let me tell you about that last threshold I helped him over. He couldn't walk very properly at his own funeral, of course, but I had him at least able to stand straight." Patrick's nostrils widened with a new wave of mind-focusing confusion. It hit him like a not-too-distant whiff of his grandmother's best smelling salts.

"Now, you're old enough to hear about funerals as well as sex, aren't you, Patrick—and all in one rainy day? My parents never mentioned sex—nor unicorns either. But, like unicorns, they must've at least half believed in sex, or I wouldn't be at least half here, half standing, half resting on me stool. I was more here when younger and stronger, of course. Still, my parents talked a lot about death and about mourning, in those days. My children have it the other way around. They speak openly about sex, almost every kind of it, but never about death, not any kind of it, and don't seem even to half believe in it. You're the generation, like mine, that should speak about both, don't you think?"

"But back to Sean O'Flaherty. Sean's wife, Maeve, wanted him laid out in his dance shoes. He was to go out extra smart and well-polished for the ladies, in lieu of filling up their dance cards yet again. But when they tied the shoes on him, a hole in one sole just stared at you hard, without blinking. Death's too much to deal with when it stares at you like that. So she brought me that shoe in a hurry, one evening, what with the neighbours coming in the next morning. No problem: a small job, and I was honoured to help an old friend. But, working on his shoe, I remembered why only one shoe had a stare on it. Sean had a bit of a drag in one foot. He came to walk more and more on one side of it. He even stood vertical by leaning quite horizontal, as though standing up while trying a fair bit of sly lying down. He did it in good humour, too. So I spent some time building up the heel of that shoe on one side. No point having Sean go, for all eternity, before the final Judge of the most innermost of our darkened insoles, not able to stand squarely and answer for himself."

Patrick left for home the next day, and didn't come back to stay with his grandparents until the following spring. Grandmother sent him straight out to the workshed. "Grandfather's a bit at a loss with himself these days. Can't find himself as quickly as he used to. Go and cheer him up."

Patrick pushed open the shed door gently, and walked in at least sideways, though not backwards, as a compromise. He felt more sure of himself these days. O'Connor was sitting at the workbench, apparently doing nothing. His mug of tea was empty, but a large sugar lump still sat beside it. To the boy, it looked as forlorn as only unappreciated sweetness can be. Patrick thought, regretfully, of Mary Heaney's sad face, the girl he'd been too shy to ask for a dance at his first school ball. "What are you working on, today, Grandpa?"

"Well, Patrick, the sun warms me from the full smile on your face! Good to see you, me boy. But are you sure you're old enough, and now tall enough too, to hear very serious talk about work?" He passed Patrick the sugar lump. "I guess I'm in favour of—what you call it at school?—the principle of inertia, now. I've not stopped to conserve energy, mind you. I'm stopped because, with the war on, there's no leather to cobble. The spare I had, I sent down to the army. Inertia's my big part of the war effort. And it takes a lot of effort, I can tell you. I'd far rather be busy at cobbling." The gills at the side of his face worked more rapidly than Patrick had seen them do before. And there seemed fewer teeth in the front of his mouth. Though they were clustered in crooked crowds at the sides, as though jostling to start riots against the rule of inertia.

As it happened, work began again for O'Connor within a few days of Patrick's arrival. With the boy to keep his grandfather company, Mrs. O'Connor walked slowly into the village. She was unable, with her rheumatism, to carry more than a small sachet of her most hopeful expression. But that was enough. She visited a number of old friends. Then a slow trickle of elderly widows made their meandering way to the workshed.

Each widow brought a bag or battered basket of old shoes, slippers or boots. Their husbands may have discarded life several years ago, but they, themselves, hadn't, until now, completely finished mourning these abandoned clogs in their wardrobes. Not long afterwards, mothers and wives of some of the young men lost in battle arrived, with similar gifts for O'Connor. As Patrick found out later, this happened all over the county. The boy had mixed feelings about these gifts, though the women hugged grandfather, and left with lighter, even if more tearful, steps, than they arrived.

Grandfather's gills moved calmly and slowly again. No sugar lump was left unappreciated. He worked, first, at unsewing the donated shoes and turning them into bootees for the small crop of babies in the village, which had arrived after the soldiers got leave. Then there were bigger shoes for the ever-growing older children. "How can you take apart a soldier's shoes, grandpa, especially Mark O'Flaherty's?" "Well, you know what it is, Patrick? I must sew old hopes back onto new lives. Otherwise, the old hopes will get lost, and the new lives get awful cold feet and chilblains."

On the last day of Patrick's visit that spring—and Patrick still remembers this—O'Connor turned to his grandson in the workshed, hammer blow suspended in mid-air by the sudden up-jet of a thought. "In troubled times, a cobbler must always put his last first." Patrick was surprised his grandfather didn't stitch on even a small smile when saying this. "Why no grin from me, then? Well, troubles can overcome most any mere pun. But we can still walk into the shed backwards, or at least sideways, can't we?" Grandfather was still seriously unsmiling, but he winked.

The Whetstone

He was at a loss what to do on this—indeed, on any—weekend. It was early autumn, near the start of the war. His mother had been called in for an extra shift at the munitions factory. His father, from the last partly-censored letter, was on his way to action in ------, "over there." John let the breeze decide what to do for him, and followed it out to the shed. He was moderately hopeful it would lead him to something interesting, so hurried to keep up.

The shed was devoted exclusively to "Things for later on." His father would throw nothing away. It was almost a religious observance. However broken, in parts, unwired, unwoven, rusty, in holes, or wholly superfluous, his father had the prophetic vision to imagine a time when these things would have some crucial use that he could not, at present, imagine. It gave him a high and regimenting sense of usefulness to save—to redeem—what was currently useless, sorting things into distinct piles and boxes. In this respect, John thought his father rather like the vicar. In Sunday services, Reverend Fox encouraged them to hold themselves at the ready for the very important "times-to-come," that seemed capable only of coming, never of having arrived. John looked through some piles of junk briefly, but found them as uninviting as any sermon.

He sat on the front steps for a while, with the latest comic he'd got from the nearby American air base. Though he could've read, he mostly looked from picture to picture. The ballooned words seemed unduly limiting. As though the characters had been unnaturally thrust into an underwater world that slowed down their otherwise fast and bold actions, so they gasped out speech in desperately de-oxygenated bubbles. The pictures always suggested to him many more things that might happen next than the bubbling dialogue ever allowed for. He felt an itch in his throat for the story to continue even beyond the familiar limits of the invasion of all possible planets and worlds.

The breeze abandoned the underwater storyline with a sudden gust, and took off for the bus stop, eager, itself, for something to happen. John stuffed the comic in his back pocket, and jumped up to follow it. His face was somehow alertly blank: watching for something to respond to, but with no idea what; nor how he'd respond to what he had no idea of, yet. As though he were a very lanky portable radio: all switched on, but searching for a channel—any channel—to tune in to.

At the bus shelter, Christmas was scything the grass verges. He'd got his nickname from the day of his birth, and from the year-long and unmelting snowdrift of white hair that looked mounded up by a gale even on windless days. He had a part-time job for the village council. Christmas was seventy years old, so John was surprised to be intrigued by him. John had tried his hand at scything last year, but had been unable to keep up with Christmas, who could cut rough grass as smooth as a golf-course for hours on end, while talking effortlessly and endlessly.

"G'day to you, Johnnie. Remember that mare I bought to breed from? Well, a disappointment, but just for now. The stud I took her to, he sniffed the air when he saw me lead her in to his field. Then he backed off to the top of that field, jumped his fence in mid-sniff, and ran off for a day. You can't match-make for horses. They decide for themselves."

After the failed encounter for his mare, Christmas scythed more often for the council. Whetstoned his blade, more, too. It kept him hopeful that, next time, with the stud, things would go as he'd planned, smoother than a golf-course. Christmas pulled out his whetstone from a red kerchief in his pocket, and drew it expertly and gently along the blade. There was a series of short, sharp, high-pitched chirps, at several simultaneously discordant tones. It was as though a hardened steel cricket were chirping steadfastly, despite the approaching frosts. There was an answering and encouraged quiet chirp from inside the hollow wall of the bus shelter.

Christmas moved off, cutting grass further down the lane, talking, beyond earshot, to whatever trees were listening. John looked at the lying truths, the truthful lies, carved or inked into the wooden sides of the bus shelter. A new one caught his eye, high above "Billy is homo is tru." It read, "I shit blue stars when I think of you." The blankness slid off his blankly alert expression for a moment. He was pretty sure who'd inked that one in: a fellow down the road who'd just won a scholarship to university. It pointed, intriguingly, beyond the tightly limited invasion of at least several possible worlds.

A bus drew up. John was about to get on, when Andrea bounced off it, as energetically and smooth-complexioned as a ping-pong ball. A girl in his class at school, she was from the next village. They'd never really talked, as talk between the sexes was outlawed, most talkatively, by the headmistress, who, in consistency, looked only at the girls while delivering this message in assembly. Andrea's legs were brown from the long summer, perhaps extra long from it, too. Not used to talking, they greeted each other with quick sideways blinks of their eyes. "Let's swap comics" was all she said, and determinedly stepped back from the road into the churchyard to do so. He followed, and their footsteps munched eagerly up the gravel path to the church porch, to be out of the growing breeze. That sound, alone, suggested more might happen than her words allowed for. Still, he touched the rolled-up comic in his back pocket for the reassurance of a fall back position.

They passed Christmas, hair drifted up more than ever, now at work trimming grass between the graves. Unconcerned whether the dead had ears for him rather than only each other, he talked on. "I've got an old Bible at home, on the shelf by me nutcrackers. Don't get read at all. But I'm sure its just being there makes a difference in the house. Like the crabapple tree planted by me father. Makes a lovely cooling shade in summer, and shelter from winds in the winter." John, more alertly aware than ever of Andrea's summer-long legs, felt the lucky penny in his pocket. If unread Bibles can influence things, why not unspent lucky pennies, too?

In the church porch, she caught his hand, and pulled them together. Her bare knees nuzzled his, with the friendliness of curious animals. The last trace of opaque blankness slid from his face, which shone with alertness alone. He put his arms around her. It was about to be ... was about to be ... his first ... Kiss? His nose began to drip in the gathering cold, and he tried to conceal it with a half sniff. It was then that they heard a very loud munching of gravel. A coffin and four bearers rounded the corner, processing straight at them. The bearers wore very hungry, very shiny, heavy black boots. One man had a beard like a long square shovel. He kept nodding meaningfully at them, digging at the air with his chin. For a split second, John had the odd feeling it must be an apparition, that he'd sniffed it into being. It seemed utterly improbable that it should actually be happening when he had a girl in his arms for the first time. Next, the boots began to move without making any noise at all, and men and coffin seemed to be floating towards them. Then he realized this was because his whole attention was being drawn back to Andrea, who was squirming with horror to get out of his tightly encircling arms.

Andrea ran along the gravel path, which circled the church, away from the procession. John followed, his face duly opaque again. The moment had been lost. Their desperately sliding feet made slurring sounds in the gravel, as though the path couldn't quite clear its throat, and nothing more would ever be definitively said, let alone done.

John's eyes were flailing, not just his arms, eager for something to catch on to. He took in Christmas having a break, and lighting his pipe beneath a yew tree. His lips were drawn back, in anticipation of a good smoke. Christmas's teeth were grouped in pairs that leaned into, and crossed over, each other, like wrestlers in a serious bout. Some wrestlers looked in danger of being thrown right out of the ring. They kept a gap in the middle, for the neutral referee of his pipe. John's eyes flailed even more, overcome by, but unable to shut out, such currently desperately unuseable detail. Then, with a single puff, Christmas disappeared inside a cloud of tobacco smoke. But he went on talking, as though issuing commandments from just beyond the very edge of the familiar and visible universe. "Run after her, Johnnie! Run!"

John caught up with Andrea behind the church, by the shed where tools and flower-vases were kept. She leaned against its door. Her legs trembled, the dimples on her knees breathing deeply. Acting entirely on their own initiative, John's arms threw themselves around Andrea. He lunged after them, to keep up, in no doubt that they were leading him beyond any previously possible worlds. Their lips touched and wriggled together briefly, like two pairs of nervous but gentle caterpillars of an extremely exotic sort. Two small breasts confided against his chest from beneath her thin sweater. They had lives of their own, and moved differently from her. They also nuzzled more expectantly than knees did. Then she slipped from his arms and ran down the path to the bus stop. Another bus was pulling in.

Christmas was still scything grass. John could hear his whetstone tirelessly at work. Its chirps soared in the cooling air over the intervening nave of the church. Two pigeons on the spire jerked their wings open, like startled prayerbooks suddenly finding their places in a brand new order of a service. There were answering and duly encouraged chirps from the other side of the toolshed's door. They picked up their rasping speed, too. John touched his lips, as if to check whether they'd changed into something extraordinary. For John, the chirps bore the promise that winter—and its silencing of all crickets—had been successfully delayed. At least until after a next meeting with Andrea.

The Horsemen

Ed and Mary O'Brien had just moved to a ninety-four acre hobby farm. They hoped this would be a step on the way to "renewing the marriage," as they sometimes put it. With the move complete, and everything in its place in the farmhouse, the huge and enduring axed rafters were unsure, that first night, whether they, or the O'Briens, were to initiate the renewal, and quite what the next step should be. Various rafters creaked anxiously in the breeze, to show willing, and waited for something to happen. But it seemed the O'Briens were unsure, too, that first evening. Apart from those odd creaks, the rooms overflowed with silence, as the O'Briens sat in facing armchairs after supper, either side of the woodstove. However, Mary did notice, as she'd begun to recently, that Ed relaxed in an oddly poised way. As if he'd sat down only in the midst of jumping up, and might resume that trajectory at any moment. Even his favourite armchair looked tensely poised, too. He seemed ready enough for transitions. Good man, she thought. He was going to work the farm after years of growing boredom running a cornerstore. She would continue in her job as a librarian.

Ed coiled even further back in his chair, as Mary rose to pull the curtains closed—though there were none but shyly voyeuristic coyotes to look in. Ed noticed, as he'd begun to recently, how, when Mary lifted both her arms, her once hesitant and unadventurous breasts now bulged aggressively, as if with a czarina's ambitions to fill whole rooms. He felt squeezed back in his chair, though he knew it was a bust as harnessed as a tightly hobbled horse. He thought of the forty untethered and unbroken horses in the paddock outside, that he'd begin looking after tomorrow, for a neighbour who wanted to breed from them. Their supper table promptly struck him as unpromisingly barren, with its full set of empty chairs.

After breakfast the first morning, a big loop of keys was much in evidence, hanging from Mary's belt. She had keys to the larder, the writing desk, the dresser drawer her side of the bed, the root-cellar, her mother's locket around her neck, hat boxes, suitcases, and, if not birds' nests in the trees outside, certainly their own unsatisfactory recent past and soon-to-be-organized future. Ed eyed the glinting, clinking mass nervously. It was as sharp-edged, as weapon-like, as a tempered steel porcupine. "I won't feel relaxed enough to sleep tonight, if you think you need to lock everything up." Ed had left the ignition keys to tractor and pick-up truck somewhere in the vehicles themselves. He would never quite remember, Mary thought, to bring them safely inside.

When he'd fed the horses, and ploughed up a kitchen garden for vegetables, Ed spend the rest of the day walking over the property and checking barns and fences. As he walked, he began to worry about things he couldn't do much about: the wet weather, insect infestations, rotting fence poles. By supper time, the soles of his feet and his patience had both worn thin with this walking form of worry. He worried, too, about his wife, and the renewal of their marriage. She'd suggested they see a marriage counselor, or even psychiatrist. He'd shot back, dismissively, "If a lady-bug, even a centipede, crawled along the arm of a psychiatrist's couch, they'd leave with a splint on each leg. And one up their asses." He'd been pleased with his reply at the time. But, now, he couldn't keep worry about their marriage separate from worries about things he knew he couldn't change. For him, his wife had become much like the weather. He greeted this thought with the surprising and unpredictable way he'd had, since a child, of clearing his nose: by widening his nostrils and snorting explosively. A large horse in the paddock snorted back, as if in shared understanding.

The horse made him think of something he'd read, in a magazine, about the age-old ruts of chariot wheels worn into the streets of the excavated Roman city of Jerash. His memories of courting his wife were like those ruts, carved firmly into his consciousness. The ruts looked as though chariots might race down them once more in the very next moment. But they wouldn't. No more than Mary would make him walk into glass doors again by jogging by in her tight pink track suit.

Whatever Mary, Ed, and the rafters in the house were waiting for, it was at sunset of that first day that something happened to Ed. He walked into the middle of the paddock, to enjoy the sun stitching Hawaiian shirts out of the sky. The horses were in small groups of three or four, around the perimeter, some lying, but one in each group standing, alert and on guard. It began slowly, so at first he didn't realize what was happening. Horses got to their feet, one after another, and the groups joined each other, trotting in a long file behind the big horse that had snorted at him.

Ed relaxed, hands in his pockets, enjoying the scene. The horses broke from trot into canter and gallop, and the circle they made around the perimeter began to close in about him, as the big horse led them in smaller and smaller circles. Then, with a flick of his tail, the lead horse ran straight at Ed, followed by a long file of flying turf, hoofs and thunder. Ed stiffened, wishing he were nothing more than a post in the ground. At the last moment, the big horse pulled up, no more than an arm's length from Ed. He shook his mane so vigorously, it looked like a second animal—a wildcat—tumbling about on his back; then neighed with bared teeth. Ed let out a laugh, from sheer relief. That was obviously the right thing to do. The horse neighed again, as if confirming that he was laughing too, then led his company quietly back to the edge of the paddock.

From that moment on, Ed felt close to the horses, that he'd passed some sort of matriculation test with them. He loved that big horse, calling him "Mike." "There's not a dishonest one among them," he told his wife, "not a single mealy-mouthed politician or carpet salesman. They show you exactly what they feel, and oh boy, do they feel a lot." It was as though Mike's charge had renewed something in him, had shown him what was inevitably and energetically coming his way, if only he stood his ground. Mike had told him as simply as any horse could, and Ed was determined to go on listening to Mike as simply as he could, too. What was supposed to be coming his way, neither he nor Mary were sure of, at this point.

Mary liked the animated change in him. But, at times, she wished she knew quite where it was going. She added more keys to her loop. The day after Mike charged him, Ed began to brew coffee, cowpoke style, in a pan in the paddock. At first, she'd go out and join him, for the company. But whatever he was doing to the coffee, it tasted terrible to her: like a mixture of tar and liquorice poured over piles of musty hay. The unbroken horses, however, always gathered around him, at a respectful distance. So she left him to them.

At the end of each day, they'd sit by the woodstove. Ed enjoyed watching the red and orange flames through its small window. They didn't so much flicker individually, as weave amongst each other with a corporate mentality, like a shoal of bright carp in an Emperor's pool. They wove about in their own, inner-driven way, whether there was a high wind outside or not. Sometimes, on the stillest of nights, they leaped the highest, as though to emphasize that the unlikely can, indeed, be the thing most likely to happen.

Ed was glad summer was ending. Many days, working the farm, he'd been badly bitten by mosquitos. But, though cooler nights were drawing on, he'd still wake up some nights, from troubled sleep, prickling all over from invasive dreams of galloping horses. In the mornings, so he'd joke to himself, he was unsure which bites on his forearms were from insects, which from his dreams. If anything, the dreams bit worse. Mary noticed a fidgety restlessness in him, which she liked a lot less than his previous quietly repressed energy.

Mary noticed quite a few changes in Ed's behaviour. At times, she thought them encouraging signs of an energetic transition to farming. At times, she wasn't so sure. The week before Christmas, she drove to various clapboard churches in the valley, to play the organ for their small congregations. It was always snowing. Ed came with her, to shovel her out if, need be. One evening, driving back from a service, they noticed horses in a nearby field, standing quietly in a circle, under the full moon, clouds of breath rising above them like frozen prayers. Ed pulled over, climbed the fence, and trudged out to them. She watched them part ranks, to make a place for him. He stood there with them, flank to flank, for several minutes, all heads bowed, clouds of breath intermingling. A glittering sight, but she wasn't sure why on earth he'd done this on such a cold night, when they weren't his horses, or in distress. And why, as unbroken horses, hadn't they shied away from him?

He often, now, openly and unselfconsciously, scratched at his crotch, right in front of her, something he'd never done before. He even did this at the supper table. Though he usually caught himself at it, and quickly converted it, in an exaggerated sweep of the arm, to scratching his nose instead. The double-decker gesture infuriated her. She'd rather he'd done neither, but, failing that, just one of them, consistently and honestly, so it was quite clear to both of them what she was complaining about. Then there was the odd way he often stomped at the ground with his boots, while sawing or digging. Was it a sign of dissatisfaction with how the work was going—something he could keep at and overcome? She began to scrape the bottom of the barrel of her imagination here, as the work seemed to be going very quickly. Dissatisfaction that he was only five foot seven, that gravity had a pull, that the blue sky was blue? She gave up.

Mary saw the house as her acreage, and tried to maintain good order there, whatever Ed got up to outside. They'd had a new stainless steel counter installed in the kitchen. At first, Ed took his part in keeping it clean and polished. Now, he complained that he had only to look at it, to leave meandering trails of eye-prints all over it. Though he still said, "I'll clean it up," he spoke as though he didn't recognize his own voice, didn't know who had said that, or why; as though he were becoming apart from himself. To counterbalance this loosening, Mary was unable to unstick the mental super-glue bonding her to her frustration with him.

Mary took on a few light jobs on the farm, like feeding the chickens early in the morning, before driving to her job at the library. One day, she was surprised when the big horse, Mike, leaned over a fence, and awkwardly, but gently, picked up the pail of feed by its handle, setting it down closer to her, so she didn't have to stretch. He then resumed cropping the grass unconcernedly, in a kind of double-decker gesture that made it seem, for a moment, that he'd been cropping all along, and the pail had somehow moved all by itself. Perhaps, just as Ed seemed to draw closer and closer to the horses, they—or Mike at least—might draw closer to what she hoped for in a helpmate. She laughed at the sheer absurdity.

One morning—around the time of the first snow—Mary woke up, bleary-eyed, to what looked like a horse's head on the pillow beside her, its mane as tousled as another sleeping animal. She seemed to make out the whole horse, under the coverlet, in bed beside her, breathing gently and twitching its tail. She was surprised at how unsurprised she felt. It didn't seem at all like waking up within a bad dream. She slid out of bed, with disgust. It was going to be impossible to keep the sheets clean, at this rate. The disgust grew into horror. Ed was nowhere in sight, though she could hear the tightly clenched sounds, white and stoccato, of an axe splitting logs. The side door had been left open, and she ran outside. Her nightdress fluttered and swirled around her like snowflakes in cottony spirals.

Ed threw down his axe, and stared at her, as she told of her waking. The cold quickly got to the muscles in her face. She felt her lips move more and more slowly and awkwardly. They moved so slowly, she had the odd impression they were actually beginning to move backwards phonetically, unsaying the very words she was trying to get out. Ed laughed, then snorted loudly. Mike did not snort back, and was nowhere to be seen, though he usually leaned companionably over the fence when logs were being split. Still, there was a streak of yellow in the fresh snow, and hoof-prints right up to the fence.

Ed reminded her of a movie they'd once seen, which had given her nightmares at the time. He led her back to the bedroom. There was certainly no horse in the bed, now. Though there was a single roan hair on the pillow. She got dressed, collecting her thoughts as she counted her keys. The key loop was a rosary for having useful insights: she would ask Ed to take more care of the straggling reddish-grey beard he was growing. But not every key offered insights now: "Why leave the side door open, Ed, so a horse might, just possibly, get in, even up the stairs to the bedroom? Stop being so trustful around animals." Ed lost control of his eyes. They looked back at her like two eggs frying at a very high heat. If eyes could spit fat at you, his would've done.

At work that day, Mary got a bad migraine headache. It locked around her forehead, tight as a spiked metal collar on a large, straining pit bull. She decided to go home early. Headaches, even if bad, were never entirely unwelcome to her. She'd developed a subtle relationship with headaches—though, incidentally, not with dogs, which she'd, quite straightforwardly, never really liked or understood. Headaches could be used to keep intrusions at bay, and more reliably than pit bulls. She'd seclude herself in bed, curtains drawn, and ask Ed to stay well away for a day or two.

When Mary drove into the farm, there was no sign of Ed. Her headache began to fade somewhat, like a carpet stain under her new cleaning fluid. No sign of him anywhere. She phoned neighbours. No one had seen him leave the farm. The truck was still in the barn, keys left, irresponsibly, on the running board. Mike was nowhere to be seen, either. One neighbour reported having seen a horse cantering down the highway, and had thought that odd: enterprising stud horses usually made off through the bush. "Looked like he was a horse with half a mind to thumb a ride." But the neighbour didn't think it was Mike.

Still, when Mary counted the horses in the paddock, she was definitely one down.

Mary looked in the out-houses carefully. Rounding a corner of the log pile, she came face-to-face with a young, heavily bearded, and rather unkept young man. He was nervous, and nearly shied away from her, but said, forthrightly, that he was looking for work as a farmhand. Said he knew horses well, and flicked a long pony tail at her, to emphasize the point. Though no one had seen him before in those parts, Mary took him on, to keep the farm going. She was sure, fingering her keys, that Ed had abandoned her. Indeed, she never saw Ed again, never knew where he'd got to, and found, fairly soon, that she didn't much care. As she told a friend, "Whatever he renewed into, it wasn't our marriage." Mike was never seen again either. He was probably caught in a distant round up, sold elsewhere in a horse fair.

Ralph, as the farmhand called himself, stayed on, working for Mary. He kept to himself, converting one barn into a cabin. He got on excellently with the horses. He had a loosely shaped, pudgy face, that seemed permanently dissolved into quickly shifting expressions. It was held together by his tight red beard, which rasped against the collar of his jacket, like a buzz saw trying, vainly, to make a good clearing in his face for one constant, angular expression.

The farmhand had hazel-green eyes. He never spoke of his past, though Mary sometimes wondered whether he wasn't wistfully nostalgic. Then, when he looked at her, shy and deferential, Mary could see a very small brown flake glint in one eye. It was like a scale on a fresh trout in the market that still looked so healthily alive, you wondered whether it might not burst into its previous unrestrained life again, in a sudden, deep dive.

Ralph grew his pony tail unrestrainedly. Mary was unnerved to see him flick it expertly at flies that were bothering him, as though he'd never had to learn or practice this. On nights with a full moon, she'd sometimes watch him, from her bedroom window, as he was out in the paddock doing a last check with the horses. He stood flank to flank with them. On misty nights, it was hard to tell where horses ended, and if a man began.

Ralph kept pretty clear of "Missus Mayri." He thought her a very odd woman. She'd once told him that her husband might as well have run off to become a horse. In her heart of hearts, she also thought—though she was too smart to tell him this—that her farmhand, of unknown origin, might just as well once have been their big horse, Mike. He seemed to continue in the same line of awkward helpfulness. But she knew her rosary of keys would offer no insights on that. She was getting better with her keys. Though she continued to notice that flames in the woodstove still often leaped highest on the most windless of nights.

A Legend

The sun was low in the sky. Arnie, the cantor, started singing the prayers to welcome the Sabbath. The rabbi was home in bed today, with a bad cold that was doing its rounds as thoroughly as a census taker. Outside the window, Arnie saw the snow reddening, mounded by the roadside like a huge pink blancmange made by one of his grandmothers. Or was it more like his throat felt: a spreading inflammation? At this point, his voice gave out completely.

Arnie whispered as loudly as a hacksaw, that someone should take over for the rest of the service. But there were no volunteers. The small congregation shuffled for warmth near the woodstove, orbiting around it like satellites in steaming gabardines. All together, they turned the page in their prayerbooks, uncertain quite where this would take them, beyond staring at a new page.

As if invited to do so by the uncertainty, the Eternal Light at the front of the synagogue began to blink off and on at irregular intervals. Izzy, a ninety-year-old veteran of the Second World War, looked up from his prayerbook with long-lasting military alertness. "It's signalling, I think. Someone's trying to tell us something. The world's going to end." Then he added, more quietly, looking with wrinkled longing across the aisle at Susanna, just turned twenty, "But new worlds keep starting up." His know-it-all son Sol replied definitively and angrily, "It's just the fuses and that wiring again." Sol gave Marty, the community's electrician, a stare like a flying snooker ball. Izzy deflected the stare with his well-practiced "You only end up on the floor if you're too damned sure." The stare wouldn't have hit its target anyway. Marty's thoughts were wrapped up in something much more than his two moth-eaten scarves.

The hacksaw voice rasped again, though more slowly, now drawn rustily through very wet and wooden words: "Can someone please, please, take over." Marty stirred uncomfortably in his seat. Everyone knew even bullfrogs in the marsh were envious of his croak when singing, so surely he wasn't going to offer his own services. Still, he was definitely worked up about something, opening and closing his overcoat nervously, so that steam from his grease-embroidered waistcoat came out in puffs, like an idling steam engine about to engage gears vigorously.

"What's up, Marty?" Izzy asked perceptively. Then Marty's words came tumbling out, as if propelled by inner pistons. "We can finish the service. With Sammy. Brought him back with me last week, from the pet store. Just took to him. His eyes seemed to follow me around everywhere. He's a big Japanese ornamental goldfish. Somehow, he knows the whole service. Don't ask me how. It sounds crazy, I know. But he did it for me last Friday. And can he ever sing beautifully!"

Well, to cut a short story shorter, when the laughter died down, they voted that Marty should fetch Monsieur Goldeynfeish forthwith. Of course, there were conflicting motives behind this unanimity—as there usually are. Sol wanted an extra chance to make fun of Marty. Izzy found parts of Marty's story utterly unbelievable, but was wonderingly open-minded about the rest. "Heck, a grown man wouldn't go out and buy a goldfish. And even if he did, he wouldn't give it a name. I ask you! Still, I reckon the universe is big enough, a fish may swim by, one day, that can sing. Let's give it a try and see. Why, if for King David, in the Psalms, hills clapped their hands, maybe for us, a goldfish will be Pavarotti."

Marty encountered some stinging rebukes from children on the street, as he walked carefully from his nearby home to the synagogue, a fishbowl held at pious arm's length in front of him. "Hey, mister, you don't take no fish for a walk!" "Hey, do little fishie do fire hydrants?" "Mister, get yourself some pet dog wid flippers!" The rebukes were followed by a few equally stinging wet snowballs. But both rebukes and snowballs slipped off his gaberdine of meekly tailored, oil-spattered perseverence.

Sammy and Marty were escorted to the front of the synagogue by most of the highly curious, bemused, amused or ribald congregation. Arnie was relieved to see that the large goldfish was attired, by nature, in a respectful skull cap of white pigmentation on the top of his head. He even wore a prayer shawl of grey colouring on his back, with long fringes that trailed behind his tail fin. In appearance, this was certainly a fish in accord with ancient tradition. But could he sing?

Marty placed the bowl respectfully on the podium, and set up a microphone and prayerbook beside it. But nobody, not even Izzy, was prepared for what followed. At first, there was a thin sound, tremulous and nervously uncertain, like a finger being run around the rim of a glass of potato vodka. Then, as Sammy seemed to gain confidence, gills fanning steadily, this modulated downwards into a clear, bell-like voice, enunciating each word perfectly, a leaping porpoise of a baritone, that dived, at times, to a huge, rumbling whale of a bass at mysterious liturgical depths.

After a minute or two, the large fish turned sideways to the prayerbook, lips moving assuredly. He no longer needed the text. It was as if he were reading prayers out of the very water in his bowl; and, as his voice grew stronger, from the water outside, dripping slowly in the guttering; from rainy sleet in the passing, ever-wandering and homeless clouds; from the half frozen puddle on the sidewalk by the door, where an alley cat lapped thirstily; from the town's creek, flowing steadily under its layer of ice; from the distant sea itself, into which all creeks flow, at the very vanishing point of both life and death.

The fish sang beautifully. Never could Arnie, at his best, have matched this Sammy Goldeynfeish. Never before had anyone in the room heard such surging, rhythmic, melodies. Song rose from Sammy's lips like shining bubbles in a great ocean of praise. As raindrops fall back into the oneness of the sea, losing their distinctness within it, so a spirit of gently merging oneness with the universe filled the room. Sol even smiled at Marty, "Oy Vey!" Though he was somewhat alarmed by this—indeed any—pleasure.

Then, suddenly, the singing stopped. Marty tried dropping fish food into Sammy's bowl, from a pouch he kept in the pocket of his still steaming gaberdine of preparedness, nestled beside a pair of pliers. Arnie's broken voice cajoled, but as unsuccessfully as any hacksaw would. Sol scowled at Marty. "Told you so. It's all a fraud, a joke. The fish was only lip-syncing. You know Marty's an electrician by trade. He just set up a record player and loudspeaker, hidden away somewhere. All we heard was some famous Russian cantor. At least the fish isn't belly up." Indeed, Sammy looked perfectly content in his bowl. But nothing would persuade the singing to start up again.

Izzy's left leg trembled with unsatisfied yearning for the many melodies of the rest of the service. He tried to recall the oceanic feeling that had filled the room just a moment ago, so that it might stay dammed up in him a bit longer. He looked at Susanna across the aisle, not a stolen, sneaked glance, but one of ninety years of wide-eyed, steady wonder. His eyes brushed her cheeks tenderly and solicitously, and then moved on in the same way over the whole congregation, including both quietly swaying Sammy Goldeynfeish and raging Sol in one continuous and unbroken movement.

In the hullabaloo that broke out, Marty escaped with Sammy to the washroom, and locked himself in. This spoiled, overfed fish needed talking to. "Samuel, how could you do this to me, you little bottom-feeding, scaly schmuck! My reputation's in tatters." Indeed, even his gaberdine looked more than threadbare in the harsh light of the naked bulb in the ceiling. It was beginning to be less of a coat, more a great and gathering host of darns, some riding piggyback on others. It was true, as his grandmothers had said, even darns need darning in this unravelling world.

"Last Friday, at home, you sang the whole service so beautifully. Don't know how you did it. But, as you did it, even if it's impossible, you obviously can. So what gives with tonight? You oughta be ashamed of yourself, for leading me on." Sammy looked entirely calm and unashamed, if that's what blowing out well-formed and tight bubbles means. He seemed to be collecting his thoughts carefully, and swivelled around in a slow but emphatic movement to face Marty.

"It's like this," Sammy began, patiently. His voice rose out of the fishbowl clearly and firmly, without the help of any microphone. "Last Friday, once you'd got over being so unnecessarily surprised, you sang along too. Didn't you, now? Tonight, no one really joined in, not even quietly and croakily, sucking on half-priced old peppermints. They were going to let me do the whole service for them. Now, you should know I'm no rabbi among fishes—that's left to the great whales. But my guess is that your rabbi, once he gets over that cold, wouldn't like it if I'd carried the whole service. Not because I'm a fish, dammit, as this is your twenty-first century, and he's wonderfully fair-minded. Besides, we're living in such equitable times, at long last. Well, aren't we? But because it would look awfully as though I'd handed you all a temptingly polished apple of song, which it was wrong of you to accept so passively. You should've tended the tree of song in yourselves.

"You just can't sing 'Yes' to Life by proxy, my buddy. I'm no bottom-feeding proxy-fish for your lot. You gotta sing 'Yes' for yourselves." There was a stream of indignant, even prophetic, bubbles. "You gotta see it from my point of view, too. That old story about a Garden of Eden, it got snakes' heads smashed in by your kind for centuries. How can I let ornamental goldfish in for that kind of treatment too?"

Marty found the discussion confusing. Still, who expects fish to argue clearly, anyway? He unlocked the washroom door, intent on getting home as quickly and unobtrusively as possible. Going down the corridor to the front hall, he noticed that they were all alone in the building. Instantly, he realized that they were locked in, with the newly installed alarm system and the hall's motion-sensor switched on. He couldn't even get to the front door to unlock it from inside, without setting off alarms in this world and the next, and all the embarrassment and expense that would involve. He'd have to stay there all night.

Marty sank to his knees in the corridor, puffs of anxious steam coming out of both his coat flaps and mouth. The temperature was dropping. Sammy tried to offer advice. "Why not curl up on a bench, and wait until morning. There's a proper time for everything: a time to get locked in at night, but a time to be let out in the morning." "Oh shut up!" retorted Marty. "I don't want no preacher-fish sermon, thank you."

"Well, why not look for another way out. Perhaps the bathroom window." Marty considered this briefly. The window was high up and small. As he remembered, the security system didn't include it. He might, indeed, get through it. But what a scrambling effort! He was already feeling very tired. What he needed was a quick fix. "Isn't there something else you can think of, Mr. Smartyscales?"

Sammy turned towards him with another slow-finned and emphatic swivel. "Slide my bowl across the floor, and see what happens. Only don't ask questions. By the way, you'll pay for this. Big time! That's the way karma always seems to go. Now, put your housekeys in my bowl." Marty complied, and pushed the bowl across the floor. Almost immediately, bowl and Sammy disappeared, and Marty found a long staff beside him. "Oops!" came Sammy's voice, apparently from nowhere, or at least somewhere quite close to it. "Old trick, sorry. Pick up the stick and throw that to the floor." Bewildered, Marty did so. Straightway, there was a cellphone sliding across the tiles were the stick had been. He picked it up in amazement, but the amazement promptly faded enough for him to dial Arnie, to come and let him out.

Marty's little house was at 145 Eden Avenue, adjoining David Street. He'd lived there, as a bachelor, for ten years. Ever since his wife had left him for a travelling encyclopedia salesman. Marty was very much a homebody, himself. But Viv had longed to see the world, even at the expense of running away with someone who often sold himself only half way through the alphabet. Unfortunately, when this new man took off, that left her with a lot of world to see that only began, abruptly and unsatisfyingly, at "M," stacked in piles of dust-covered volumes in her spare room. For her, that was too big a jump to make, so she stayed put, and tried to be happy with just yearning to travel. Meanwhile, Marty had buffered himself from whatever strange and incomplete alphabets the world might throw at him, leaving his house only for work, shopping and worship. So it was with a feeling of great security that he let himself and Sammy back into his home. He had to retrieve his house keys from the fishbowl to do this. But he replaced them immediately afterwards, as Sammy and his water were becoming very agitated. Then, after putting the fishbowl on the table, he promptly fell into deep goose-feathered dreams and his mattress.

He overslept the next morning, and had to leave for work in a funnel-shaped cloud of a hurry. As he whirled out to his car, he made sure to throw feed into Sammy's bowl. No time to talk with him about the previous night. Besides, how crazy to talk with a fish! He'd have to put a stop to that, or he'd be more than a laughingstock with Sol. It was a long day of work, with clients to visit who had tricky wiring problems. When he pulled back into the driveway, he couldn't find his house keys in his pocket. Then he remembered he'd left them in the goldfish bowl, and the door must be unlocked. But the door wouldn't open. He tried it again. It was locked after all. He couldn't understand it. It was like waking up only to find yourself in yet another dream about trying, unsuccessfully, to wake up.

Then Marty's neighbour, Joe, ran across from his driveway, his crew cut bristling with carefully bleached excitement. "Marty, I gotta tell yer, some huge moun'ain uv a bag lady, she go inter yer howse wid her shoppin' trolley. She gotta feishbowl wid goldeynfeish init, and lotsa bags o' tuff. And three cats foller her in too. Real nice follerin' kinda cats." Then they both tried the door and rang the bell, for over half an hour, but got no response. All the curtains were closed, so they couldn't see in. It was dark already, and getting colder. The sky began to run a black-and-white movie about heavy snowfalls. Marty felt tired and distant from it all, and begged a spare bed for the night in Joe's house.

The following day was a frustrating one for Marty. His lawyer advised him to arrange to rent an apartment, just in case. It could be a long process, getting his house back from a squatter. That was just the way the law had gone, in those parts. And the house wouldn't be in good condition, even then. Marty spent most of the day following the lawyer's advice. Late in the afternoon, he took a break in a coffee shop. His hands seemed as glazed as his eyes at this point, and the cup slipped and spilled coffee over the only pair of pants currently available to him in the universe. He thought of the two spare pairs in his small oak wardrobe at home. Marty tried to recall a proverb, to help himself be stoical. This was definitely the last camel that was going to break any more of his straws.

He drove to his house, and banged relentlessly on the door, prepared to continue until either the door opened, or his hands fell off. The door opened surprisingly quickly. The bag lady just stood there, hands folded calmly behind her. Though he tried to push in, she barred the way effectively, just by filling the doorway. Her creased blue dress was obviously well-trained to expand into every available space. He pushed again. She brought out her hands from behind her, propelling him backwards down the steps. Each hand held an immense and quickly twirling fly swatter. There was no way he would ever get back into 145 Eden. As he walked down the driveway, he heard a beautiful baritone voice sing out through a categorically closing door.

Banking by Mirrors

I

I SHOULD TELL YOU NOW, I was a horse trader all my working life. So you may think this is a colt with a slight limp I'm trying to sell you. But you'll see very well for yourself, if you hold the halter on this story, and walk it about.

Town council was all for the bank's plan to put up a new building. It was to be ten stories high, with plenty of office space; one of those steel and glass things that looks like a giant, four-sided, free-standing shaving mirror. Some of us from the seniors' home raised objections. For myself, I couldn't see the point of any mirror that big. But we were as good as told we were already up to our waists in each other's graves, and couldn't be expected to move about with the times. I ask you, what does a town, with a population of a little over three thousand, need a building like that for? Now, water-pipes to the outlying houses, or another brewery, that's a different matter. The old bank building, in a converted mill, had done just fine. It kept your money as fresh and as free from weevils as any sack of flour.

Anyhow, the bank's new building went ahead. In horse trading, you need to keep up with things. So I rolled my misgivings up in a thick wad, and swallowed them down with my tea. That was until I met up with an old friend of mine, who'd retired to the big city. In his younger days, he could've sold you a brood mare with no nipples on her, and you'd have thanked him for it. He was canny, all right. He told me about the big bank buildings near where he lived. It seemed some funny things had been happening. He reckoned the same would happen in our town too, though it might take an eye trained on horses to notice it at first. Given the tip-off, I pinned back my eyes and just bided my time.

II

Can't say I noticed much going on while the building was under construction. But it was surrounded by hoardings that would've kept anything in. Even horses tampered with by skunks couldn't have kicked through. Then one wet morning, the hoardings were down. I'd seen nothing quite like it. At first, it was a brand new bit of the sky, though with some peculiar weathers of its own. Clouds crawled over all ten stories of it. As the storm built up, they seemed to boil out of the top of it, foaming down its sides like a badly poured truck of beer. Later, as the sun came out, the clouds dissolved into the shutters, presumably re-herding the other side of them. So it went on for the rest of the day, with clouds busily going in and out of the building. The new bank seemed nothing more than a great goddam warehouse of storms. You wondered how many clouds they could possibly keep piled up in the vault inside. Still, if this was moving with the times, it was no stranger than packing horses inside a shiny steel transporter, and driving them to the horse fair, with not an honest hoof beat heard along the way. This was only the beginning, though.

The first day the bank was open for business, I happened to be up early and out for a walk. There the building was, shamelessly hanging up its multi-storied mirror under any passing cloud. There were acres of glass there, enough for a profitable small farm. Every acre was bright and alert, though it was only just after dawn. Without waiting for the tellers, they'd gone into business on their own: collecting reflections from the town, and taking in everything that happened, too. Nothing was too large or too small for their prompt attention. The day's first bus drove by me, a bit too close to the curb. I saw it deposited instantly, with a flex of quicksilver, up on the shutters at the second floor, along with a small but bravely protesting lady. It was Mary. I was hoping to bump into her. She hadn't slept well either. As we took a turn around the building, it seemed to me that, in about two minutes flat, the entire town was impeccably transferred onto its sides. It was then that I wondered what there was left for a mirror that large and accomplished to do.

I was back for a walk again that same evening. The walls of the bank didn't knock off after normal working hours. They were still at it. Obviously, they didn't get tired and weren't yet satisfied. They just kept going, sieving out street lamps and car headlights without any difficulty. Even that early on, I saw them suck away the glint in a tomcat's eyes. He was a wary, battle-scarred cat, that one. We reckoned he'd fought his way through both World Wars, on the home front, he looked that distinguished. But he never even noticed what happened to him, it was done with such surgical precision. Now cats are one thing, but young women are definitely another. At first, I thought my eyes were playing up. The doctor's been at me for years to invest in some glasses. But I swear I could see the bank taking the love-light right out of the young girls' eyes, as they came out of the cinema. There it was, little warm pulsating beads of light, shimmering and skipping excitedly about, nearly a third of the way up the building. Though I've not lived an entirely perfect life myself, that was going a bit too far. I started wondering what I could do about it. I didn't know that things would get worse still.

III

I began hanging around the bank building most days, to see what was going to happen to the town. It was something useful to do again. To tell the truth, retirement looks good only when you're the other side of the fence from it. I'd even started to envy the glue they make old horses into. It was an excuse to see more of Mary, too. She lived in her own home, with a daughter, and was the same age as me, seventy-five. We gave the benches by the bank a good sitting on, that summer.

I took Mary into my confidences about the bank building. She'd worked around animals most of her life, until her husband had died and the farm been sold up. So I reckoned that if there was anything to notice, she'd see it all right. I suppose it's because animals don't speak up for themselves. You grow a sharp pair of eyes to notice everything about them. Buildings aren't so different from animals that way. I've only known one building that ever spoke up for itself. Mind you, I'd had some whisky first. But that's another story.

It was a relief, I can tell you, when Mary agreed with what I saw. If my eyes were loony, hers were too. Yet she still didn't need glasses at all. And it wasn't just our eyes playing us tricks. We both agreed, if you stood close by the building, and were as quiet and still as a colt daydreaming in the clover, you could feel with your whole face how the windows were working on you. There was a funny sort of updraft, and you could sense the reflections being peeled off your face. After a while, you felt as if your cheeks were pared down almost to the bone.

That wasn't all. Those windows weren't made of clear glass, the way the good Lord meant windows to be. They were a peculiar bronze and orangey colour, like a jar of my grandma's peach preserve that once took fright in a heat wave, and went badly off. As you looked at the towering walls, and the whole small town teeming away up there in a richly bronzed technicolour, it made you feel a petty, pale, undersized and insignificant part of things. It was as if you were the reflection, perhaps in someone's cracked and dusty parlour mirror, and the real town was up there, on the sides of the bank. Mary took to wearing an apricot-coloured make-up, so as to feel less reflected.

Not long after this, the bank windows intensified their business, and began to show their true colours. I sometimes had a drink with Al, in the town's only tavern. He was in the seniors' home too, and like me had never married. He was a hard one to get close to. In his young days, he'd been the fastest pig castrator in the county. But he'd liked the job an unpleasant lot, and had boasted about it. Those gloated-over pigs from the past came back to haunt me, when I tried to tell him about the bank. So I shut up, and worked on my beer instead. I didn't quite trust him. Giving me a reputation in the seniors' home for going crazy would've been his equivalent to castrating me at world-record speed. Anyhow, one day, all on his own, he started telling me how he'd noticed this reflection of his, with a fantastic Florida tan, floating above him on the first floor of the bank. Best tan he'd had in his life, he told me, laughing. He'd never felt so fit. I still couldn't open up to him, though. A week later, I wished I had.

Al sat down beside me, and ordered his usual, but there was a funny, fixed look on his face. His jaw had gone tight and self-conscious, like a man who's just asked himself a question he doesn't care to answer. He told me that, walking past the bank on his way to the tavern, he'd looked up to watch his reflection, and it hadn't been there. He'd stopped out of curiosity, walked backwards and forwards, peering more closely to see what had happened. But the windows were the same as before. He looked more worried than curious. He was going to say something more about it when he all of a sudden put his hand on his chest, and said, in a very polite voice, "Jeez, my heart's stopped!" Then he slowly keeled over in his chair, glass still in hand, beer going everywhere. I'd heard of men saying their hearts had stopped, and then falling down. But those had been natural deaths, with no windows involved. It was a big shock to me, especially as Al was only my age, and, like me, had had a healthy working life out of doors.

Mary and I were both agreed. It looked as if the bank building, having stowed away reflections from every part of the town, was now turning the tables on us. It was trying to take charge. It was going to do all the living, on a large and beautifully bronzed scale; and we were being cast out as its pale reflections. Judging from Al's case, it was going to do all the dying as well as the living. But this was not much consolation. We'd heard of international bankers' plots before, but this one capped them all. As if controlling our money and lives wasn't enough, they now wanted to be our lives. Something had to be done about it. Mary knew someone who worked as a secretary in the mayor's office. We decided she should talk to her about it. As Mary lived in her own home, with a daughter who already thought she was crazy, and loved her for it, she had nothing to lose.

I remember so clearly that afternoon when I was waiting on one of the new benches by the bank for Mary to come back from the mayor's office. The light had a strange shining quality to it that I couldn't quite put my finger on. The building seemed to be gathering the light in behind my back, and manipulating it in some complicated way, intensifying it. Mary was late. In the end, it wasn't Mary, but her daughter, who walked up and sat down by me, touching me gently on the arm. Mary had been hit by a car while crossing a road, and had a broken leg. She was now in an ambulance, going into the city. She's been on her way to the town hall at the time.

It suddenly came back to me how Mary had been commenting recently on a row of bevelled windows at about the third story of the bank. She could see all the traffic on the road in them, migrating by over her head. I'd known which windows she meant, all right, but hadn't seen anything in them myself, just more hard light. I'd put it down to the differences in our heights. She had the advantage of women whose roots stretch back to Wales. She nestled up at you from under wherever your horizon happened to be, even when you were sitting down together. It seemed to me now that the bank windows were on to us. They'd got wind of her plan to go to the town hall, and had taken precautions. I tried telling it all to Mary's daughter, but it didn't come out very well. She though I was in shock, walked me back to the home, then drove off in a hurry to meet her mother at the hospital.

IV

I'm not sure whether things have got better or worse since Mary was hit. My doctor has me on these tablets. He had the nerve to tell me I might have had a mild stroke. That was after I'd opened up to him and tried to tell him about the new bank. What a slap in the face. Something's confusing things all right. But it's not me. It's that bank. You'd think he'd know the difference between a man and a fancy bit of engineering, with all his training. Probably drinks too much. His nose blazes away like a fire in a granary. He's not taking me in, though. It wasn't often I got sold a consumptive mare, I can tell you. So I feed his damned tablets down my toilet. May it do it some good. It's been getting forgetful enough lately, not flushing properly.

The bank seems to have moved into another phase of its operation. I'm still keeping a watch on it. You might wonder what else it could do, after transferring the whole town onto its sides. Well, the windows didn't seem able to switch themselves off. They kept hustling for custom. Neighbouring windows had no choice but to eye and plunder each other, with their usual shining efficiency. On Mondays, after pegging up rows of wet washing from the backyards opposite, they just go on stealing the same pair of red longjohns from each other. Those longjohns get miraculously multiplied into the long deep streak of a perpetual sunrise. Sometimes I think this is a hopeful sign for the town. Perhaps the windows are doing the equivalent of eating each other, and the whole thing will chew itself to a stop. But sometimes I manage to be more realistic.

With two sunrises going on each Monday morning, it's getting harder and harder to tell which is which. In the distant back of my head, I know that Fred Johnson pulls one sunrise on, after it's dried and been ironed by his wife; and that the other needs no introduction at all, being an interplanetary phenomenon. But I'm darned if my eyes can pick out much difference. And I've got myself glasses too. Even the birds seem confused, and keep up their dawn song half the day.

I reckon that the difference between reflections and their things has somehow been torn out, right down to the taproot. It's gone the same way as the horse-drawn plough and the scythe my father used. I don't envy today's kids. What a confused world to grow up in. It's affecting people in our town already. These winter mornings, I can see sleepy pedestrians wavering away in the grey air, uncertain, despite several mugs of coffee, whose reflections they are. They seem unnaturally hunched over, too, to avoid being instantly decapitated by the concrete around the window frames. Twice already, my left leg has gone all stiff and useless. I've felt it shatter into sharp slivers of glass, as it hit one of those potholes that the town council has denied for years are really there. I'm not bothering to tell the doctor. Last time I saw him, after he'd been out of town for two weeks, his face was a horrible orangey-brown. That man's gone and joined the windows outright, with no shame at all. I'll fight it to the end. Old horse traders might just make it through. They've spent a lifetime saddling up the difference between the fixed and the fine-fettled. That ought to help.

REMEMBERING

I

AFTER HE'D DRESSED, Rolly Wingman sat in the wicker chair by his bed for a moment. Strangely, the chair didn't creak at all this morning. But, even though he kept perfectly still, various unknown and unnameable joints in his body struck up entirely on their own initiative, chanting a muffled *a capella* morning chorus. He listened, almost with enjoyment. Living in a downtown apartment, that was the best morning chorus you'd get.

He'd had a broken night's sleep. The old refrigerator in the kitchen had hummed and knocked all night, like a rusty freighter perpetually leaving port and bucking out to sea. Every so often, it would shudder, as though in anticipation of approaching some exotic tropic that, in his half awake mind, had seemed to be the tropic of broccoli or the one remaining bag of milk, light streaming on the water every time someone opened a porthole or door.

In the bathroom, another, but not entirely unfamiliar, face looked back at him from the mirror. "So what're you doin' here, buddy? You look far older than seventy-eight." He started shaving it anyway. After a small cut on the chin, it turned into his own. Though the hands in the mirror seemed someone else's at times, going off in different directions.

Bringing in the day's newspaper, he cautiously compared the day's date with the calendar in the kitchen. Who knows what day may creep up on you unawares? He'd had several experiences recently where tomorrow had arrived even before yesterday; and, once, two days had arrived, rather competitively, at the same time. There was a large red circle around today's date. He must clean the apartment this morning, before his wife got back. She'd been gone quite a while. Some days, he missed even her breath in the room.

Isabel had wanted to take an exotic trip. By sea, not, against all the ladylike and convent-schooled laws of nature, by air. She'd developed a strange wanderlust to see places before they got any older. He wondered, now, why hadn't he gone with her this last time.

He could almost smell the sea this morning. Or was it his sweaty undershirt? He opened a window. Only the distant smell of oily sludge in the estuary below. He tried to recall which dock she'd sailed from. But it was only a blur of many sailings he'd seen in the past, as a young docker and then Able Seaman, waving off frigates, destroyers and liners. It had always struck him as odd how the flank of a big liner can look just like the stands in a big baseball game, crowded with excited people gesticulating back. As though he and the other people on the dock were the real centre of attention, in some exotic game or event they were taking part in, unawares. As though those on the dock were going to get the biggest adventure of all.

Looking into the lounge, he was surprised that his wife's slippers, which he'd found the evening before, and put in the hall ready for her, had moved under the coffee table. They'd been hard to find, not so much packed away as apparently forgotten, at the very back of the larder for some reason. The slippers raised their head. They needed feeding. "Aha, I'd forgotten about you, Puss. Nice of my son to bring you around yesterday for company." He was relieved to find the slippers still in the hall. But a feeling drifted over him, as vague yet as impenetrable as a gathering sea fog, that he might've misplaced or forgotten something else, too. He just couldn't remember what. He thought of having a good look around the lounge right then. But how do you look when you don't know what you're looking for?

There was a spider on the floor in the corner of the hall. He picked up one of his wife's slippers to swat it. But, at the last moment, he stopped. The spider watched him steadily, holding its ground comfortably and almost in a comradely way. He wondered whether the hall looked more orderly to it, through its many-faceted eyes. Several pairs of muddy outdoor shoes lay scattered around, like cockroaches or large bed bugs caught in the glare when a light snaps on. Yes, with his wife away, he'd begun to live like an untidy bachelor. Tidying up to do. But best to leave the spider alive, to offer a kinder, multi-faceted second opinion, if Isabel were hard to please.

II

At breakfast, his entire bowl of cereal somehow got sprinkled with that blandly elusive feeling that he'd, but only perhaps, forgotten something. He didn't like the taste, and it was in every single spoonful. Maybe it was a prescription that needed picking up. One pill box—was it his or Isabel's?—was open and empty, like oyster shells stripped of their pearls.

The kettle didn't boil, to make coffee. He found it wasn't switched on. Two minutes later, a flickering flame shone through the plastic sides of the kettle. Confused, he wondered, for a moment, whether the flickering was in morse, and tried to read it. He'd been good at that in the Navy, and had kept it up. Was water evolving into a new form of signaling consciousness? But he hadn't filled the kettle, which now smouldered with indignation. He'd get a coffee at the cornerstore.

In the store-cum-pharmacy, there was no prescription in his name to pick up. He ordered coffee and a muffin, prompted by an aroma of baking as enticing as any offshore breeze from a banana plantation during his Asian tour of duty. A cornflake crumb on his chin cheekily reminded him that he'd eaten already. "But oh so what."

Sitting by the store window, he looked back at the apartment building on the other side of the road. There was a light on in his kitchen window. He wondered whether he was still up there, trying to remember what he'd forgotten, or to boil an empty kettle. He smiled sympathetically, and waved. Perhaps he up there could see him down here. But no one came to the apartment window. "Unfriendly bugger. Pity it's me."

Traffic built up outside as the morning wore on. The road was invaded, almost jostled aside, by a never-ending herd of bumper-to-bumper metal wildebeest, on their daily migration. He thought of his shore leave as a young man, in Africa. He eventually achieved the far side of the road. Some sailors passed him on the sidewalk, in a hurry to get back to their ship. Caught up in the after draft of their broad shoulders, he followed, his loose coat billowing him forward like a Sherlock Holmes under full sail.

Up a side alley, he caught sight of a small black rat walking by daintily, carrying a torn white paper bag. Church bells tolled for matins. It looked a bit like an underfed nun. A large black rat scurried after, wide hips waggling. A priest late for service? He began to follow them down the alley. Was it making confession that he'd forgotten to remember? He put that thought out of his head. Isabel was the one interested in church, and he hadn't been since she'd left. "And anyhow, how can even many gods remember all of us? And which are cats, which slippers, throughout the entire universe?"

The nun-rat dropped her bag while trying to climb a fence. Caught up in the small and fascinating drama of that instant, as he was more and more able to be, these days—he thought of it as a late-developing gift—he picked up the bag. Her companion sat on rather muddy and sullen hips and stared. The nun had been carrying a kosher hotdog. She reappeared on the fence top, shimmying along vigorously, like someone's sister Kate at an interfaith peace-rally he'd gone to as a young man. Or perhaps she was shivering, as another brisk breeze of sailors ripped by on the sidewalk. He instantly felt cold and disoriented by his absorption in this side alley of the present moment. Where on earth was he going? He turned around, saw a corner of his building, and headed back home.

III

Back in his apartment, Rolly assembled the vacuum cleaner, wondering where to begin. He stood at the ready, like the well-drilled Able Seaman Wingman who'd first flirted with Isabel. The floor stayed calm and steady. But no command came. The cat stood transfixed, watching something behind his left ear. He turned around, but saw nothing. The cat went on staring fixedly. Did the cat think it could see a past occupant of the place, one of those Molloys he'd heard so much about? Or a future one, maybe one of those Makis, who kept on asking him whether he'd thought of moving out? "Why don't you get outta here and leave me alone, Molloy or Maki. Whichever you are. After all, I'm the one paying the damn bills." Recently, he'd tried to think more clearly about the past and future. And to enjoy the sheer leisure of talking to himself.

While vacuuming, he accidentally turned over a corner of the rug from Turkestan. The underside showed the same pattern, but so much paler through the thin canvas backing that it almost dissolved into a drab jumble. He looked at the dishes piled up in the sink, and the old newspapers strewn over the floor—as though the daily press were entirely deciduous and subject to fearsome gales. The underside of the rug fitted the apartment's muddle better. "Who says which side of a rug must be up, which down?" He almost felt like conceding the place to the alternate and companionable pattern of a jumble. "Bet Molloy and Maki agree with me, don't you, me boys? Though it must be the both of you who're getting so much dust under the rug."

He ought to have the place ready for Isabel by tomorrow. He wasn't sure of the exact date of her return—couldn't find the folder of travel itineraries they always kept. But he felt sure he half-remembered—even if he'd half-forgotten—it must be around now, allowing for wind and tides. After all, there was the red-circled date on the calendar. And, talking of red, he must water Isabel's geraniums before he forgot that too. The flowers had lost their rich and velvety sparkle, and were beginning to look like the faded pink lipstick of some night before, ready to flake and peel off.

From next door, he could hear a TV channel only they seemed to get. He couldn't make out a word. But the intonation of the voices sounded fascinating and deeply pertinent. But pertinent to what? he wondered. He must ask them what channel it was. However, they kept pretty much to themselves. Now he thought of it, he couldn't remember ever meeting them.

IV

The door-bell rang with an uncertain and interrupted buzz. As though whoever was pressing it was only falteringly there. When he opened the door, his son walked in, slowly and deferentially. So slowly and deferentially, it was almost as though he'd started leaving while still arriving. Rolly took it as an unduly exaggerated form of respect of son for father, but was pleased nonetheless. He hugged him, ensuring that both were fully arrived.

While his son sat down in Isabel's armchair, he walked around the lounge, tapping down the corners of carpets. "Looking for something, Rolly?" "No. But I might as well be looking for tomorrow. Or yesterday. Or Molloy or Maki, somewhere behind my left ear." "Whaa?" Robert began to tap his right foot quietly but quickly on the floor. Rolly sensed a slight discomfort in his son, perhaps the beginnings of impatience. He thought of the fast and stuttering morse messages from his time in the Navy. If Robert was signaling something important to him, he couldn't decipher it at that speed.

He sat down opposite his son. Robert looked older, harder to recognize. But perhaps a little like he himself did in that fortieth wedding anniversary picture beside them. Rolly had the distinct feeling of sitting opposite a reassuring version of himself. "I bet me over there, being younger, remembers Isabel's schedule by heart, and the exact minute she docks." "What's that, Rolly?" Rolly hunched himself together. He knew he could sometimes get a bit confused about which chair or life he was sitting in. That had happened before, at parties. He kept his head down, stroking and straightening each finger in turn, very carefully, as though preparing to work the combination of an extremely difficult-to-open safe, and unsure what was inside it to start with.

Rolly decided to be straightforward with his son, and unburden his feelings for once. "I've really missed Isabel." "I know, Rolly.

I have, in my way, too." "I'm so looking forward to her coming back. Hope she had a good voyage." The morse foot-tapping accelerated wildly. Robert was jerking his whole leg from the thigh. "But Rolly, she died last year, about this time. I marked it on your calendar. Father Jebusnik conducted the service. Remember, that's where we first met."

Rolly looked wildly around the room. "I'm Miguel from the apartment next door, though we don't often bump into each other. You once told me I looked a bit like your son Robert." All the carpets seemed, confusingly, upside-down. He looked out the window. The grey day might be clearing. But, peculiarly, the clouds seemed to be stationary, while the patches of blue between them scudded by quite rapidly in the wind. Down below, houses on the other side of the river rippled by, windows flashing wildly, while the river stayed stubbornly still. He wasn't sure what was moving, what not. A man was eating in the cornerstore across the road. The man waved up at him. He waved back this time, absently. He stopped straightening out his fingers one by one. The safe wasn't worth opening. It was empty.

Shadows

With more time on his hands, he sometimes asked himself, what's it like to be a hill? His house was built tightly into the side of a hill. In summer, this gave all the rooms the coolness of underground watercourses; in winter, the earth's own musky body heat, with a slight brown perspiration beading the walls. The hill was quiet and undemonstrative, as his only next-door neighbour. Perhaps their two lives were much alike. The hill had the regular seasonal habits of a retired bachelor. Birds in its trees usually sang quietly. It was introverted as hills go, thickset, and perhaps a trifle melancholy, even on the brightest of days. After the clear-cutting, it was bald on top.

As the sun set on the far side of the hill, the house went dark, suddenly and completely; though the surrounding fields of corn still waved swelling ears of light. He watched the shadow of the hill spreadeagle out further and further across the fields. The house, of course, cast no separate shadow of its own. Neither did he, as he sat in the small garden. They were both instantly swallowed up in the dense black identity of the hill. It was like sinking, without trace, into a vast vat of molasses.

He went to his desk, and switched on the fluorescent lighting. As a watch repairman, he'd worked by such lighting for many years, until his retirement last week. He liked its unblinking, white, unforgetting stare. It added no distracting extra presence of its own. Not like the yellow light in other people's homes, that poured out, viscously as wood glue, through tasseled, dusty and embroidered lampshades, from morosely hidden 100 watt lightbulbs. Rather, at the flick of a switch, watch parts jumped, simply and alertly, with no moody complications, into their full and detailed presence under his lens. His whole house had flourescent lighting. He'd always been fastidious about lights.

As a transition into retirement, he'd brought home the watches of several neighbours, promising to clean and repair them. That had kept him occupied for just two days, as he'd worked with his usual quick efficiency. Now, for this evening, he was reduced to opening the case of his own watch, which kept perfect time, and had been cleaned by him only last month. He sat at the desk in his usual manner: leaning forward on the edge of the seat, exactly balanced on the very tips of the toe-nails of both slippered feet. He believed in sitting on your tip-toes at work, as exactly balanced as main wheels, ratchets, hair-springs and pinions should be. He also generally sat on tip-toes at the rare social events he attended: as ready to leave as to stay. The springs and regulators of meetings and partings could be best attended to in this way.

His watch was in perfect working condition. Perhaps, in a year, the light oil on the main spring would get sludgy, making time pass more slowly and thickly. Eventually, time can even completely congeal. For now, all he could do was admire the coordinated movement of gleaming parts. Teeth on different wheels meshed perfectly with each other, urging the long evening forward at the correct pace. Their fit with each other was as tight and right as his house with that bachelor of a hill.

He snapped the case of his watch closed, and strapped it back on his wrist. With no more watches to repair, he reached for a novel, still sitting, with precision, on the very brink of his toe-nails. After a few pages, he pushed the book aside. Clearly, the story could end this way, that way, or still another way; and a number of alternative future actions lay before the hero. The hard fluorescent light could reveal nothing definite in what was going on. He tried a jigsaw, but the light revealed, after an hour, that there was one piece missing. He looked at the phone. But the light revealed only that someone might, or might not, call. He felt confused, with no idea how to recalibrate the evening. He decided to visit an old colleague, who'd retired a year before. Perhaps he could pick up some tips.

The door to Adam Fisher's apartment opened at his third knock. He always counted these things. Surprising, how dimly lit it was inside. No fluorescent lighting here. It was as though the door had been swung open by the partial eclipse of a person. However, his nose adjusted more quickly than his eyes. He made out the faintly remembered smell of Sarah Fisher's smile: dish-washing soap, hard-boiled eggs, mothballs and eau de cologne. "Paul! Paul Ziff's arrived, Adam." Her voice began with a slight shine, but quickly went flat, like poorly applied nail varnish. She wore a purple dress. A string of ivory-coloured beads around her neck grinned spontaneously and generously, but failed to influence the tight curve of her lips, which was more of a twitch than a smile. As she led him into their living room, he noticed her red stiletto heels. Not a good fit, as she slipped slightly from side to side in them, like his father's fishing boat threatening to make heavy weather. Perhaps an over-stretched pair she treasured from her past. However, he was struck by the determined precision and control with which she kept her poised balance on their remarkably high heels. As though she could, at this point of her life, at any moment, in one decisive step, just you wait and see, live her life securely atop a towering pillar, like a tall, slim, ascetic stylite.

In contrast, Adam, in his easy chair, was as four-square as a bulging, belt-bound cabin trunk. Adam wore a loose-necked T-shirt. A thicket of grey chest hair more vaulted than struggled out, just below his neck. Then there were blue boxer shorts and green slippers. "Hey Paul! Gooda see ya! Wanna shot o' rye? Siddown now." As Adam rose to greet him, Paul was taken aback by four, even five shadows, rising to greet him too, cast by different standard lamps and wall lights around the room. There was a shadow in front of Adam, behind him, to his left, even above him on the ceiling. Paul juggled with all five proffered hands, and shook one of them disconcertedly.

As they talked over old times at Robert Brown's Jewellers, Paul was intrigued by the different lighting in their home. Apparently, Adam had been only too glad to give up watch repairs in that perpetually brightly lit back room at the jewellers. For precisely that reason, there was no fluorescent lighting in their apartment. Here, dark amber electricity spilled out from thick lampshades, like old chip fat, even heavy motor oil. It was hard for it to seep through the very thickest of the lampshades. It sometimes barely moved across the room. Adam explained how he'd put lights, chairs and small tables in different places around the room, for their favourite activities: here to play cards, there to use the phone, there to read the newspaper, over there to watch two blue fish in the small aquarium. Both fish stared back without expression, unsure what their favourite activity was supposed to be. Sarah quietly brought canapes from the kitchen while they talked. She didn't join in the conversation. Paul had the impression that conversation with her husband was one of the things that, like a true ascetic, she'd gratefully renounced. She had an even quieter presence in the room than the fan in the ceiling, which at least tapped and hummed softly.

Though Adam slouched in his armchair, T-shirt rucked up, boxer shorts rucking down, he chatted away in alert, clipped tones. Words seemed to have been dying to get pronounced by him. His tongue maneuvered skillfully around shifting and clumsy dentures. Words were frequently interspersed with clicking sounds, as his dentures made breaks for it, as though English were being simultaneously translated into Kalahari bush language.

The upshot was that he advised Paul to try Howie's Lighting. "Get rid of that (click) all-fluorescent lighting you let rule your goddam (click-click). Life. Put in different kinds of lighting around a (click-clack) room. With chairs in different (click-clock-clack). Places. And chuck out that old (clicketty-clock) repair desk. The one you brought back from (click-click) Brown's. There's life out there. (Click) grab it!" And he shoved a fistful of canapes into his mouth. Paul was skeptical. All the same, he'd learnt much from Adam about diagnosing problems with antique grandfather clocks. He took a respectfully small sip from his rye, and agreed to try it.

Paul spent the next two weeks changing the lighting in his house. Howie's Lighting couldn't have beaten him off with a luminescent stick, though his persistent questioning sometimes made them wish they could. At first, things went well, and he kept very busy. He didn't often consult his much-loved Elgin watch. Though he knew its hands were still keeping, by his measurements, to their regular and constant performance: the balance-wheel vibrating, as he kept reminding himself, 30 times each 6 seconds, and 157,680,000 times a year.

In what began as his all-fluorescent house, only the lighting in the bathroom was left serenely unchanged. He carefully positioned standard lamps, vase lamps, globe lamps and pillar lamps in various spots around the living room, a chair and a table by each. He imagined what he'd get into the habit of doing, in each place. He regretted being just too busy, organizing his future retired life in the living room, to try out any of the activities right away. Apart from sitting down, at the end of each day's work, which included some tricky electrical rewiring, to look at the view down the hill. Then he'd relax, with a cup of self-regulating mint tea in hand.

There was a tree outside the window, which often had a flock of birds in it. Aren't birds supposed to tweet? He'd always thought so. But now that he actually listened to them, they shouted loud, open-beaked "aaaahs" at each other. It sounded more like the government on TV. Everyone interrupting everyone else's interruptions, in noisy assertions about assumptions about each other's mere impressions. He'd absolutely no idea what allegedly outrageous developments, in the surrounding calmly rippling cornfields, could justify the birds' agitation. He closed the triple-glazed window impatiently, just to keep their rowdiness out.

With enough lights in the room, correctly positioned, Paul's ever-multiplying shadows became sufficiently faint and submissive. So he didn't feel about to bump into and trip over them, as he walked around. Initially, he'd spilt a few cups of tea that way. And he'd always been such a steady person. But it was only when he'd got the meekness of shadows just right, curbed their aggression, that the trouble really started.

It was when he'd driven into Edmonton to tell Adam how good his advice had been. They went for a walk in the neighbourhood park. It was a sunny fall day. Sarah was spring cleaning. "With Sarah, spring cleaning is the only season," Adam grunted. As they stood reminiscing by the duck pond, Paul was surprised to notice that his tall shadow, in the setting sun, seemed decidedly fainter than Adam's cabin trunk of a shadow. He rubbed his eyes. It was true. It stayed true even when he managed to change positions with Adam, under the pretext of brushing dead leaves off his shoes.

Later that evening, Paul removed two chairs and vase lamps from his living room. He'd never really liked chess anyway. When he tried playing chess against himself, Black and White were soon sullenly unanimous in hating the game. And he used the phone so seldom. He hardly needed a separate chair and lamp to take unwanted calls about unimaginable products from unlocatable call-centres. He was not displeased that his shadows grew more assertive. Anyway, he'd soon get used to negotiating his way between them, with one of his mother's original bone china tea cups. And, indeed, he did. But then the shadows changed their tactics.

He noticed it most late in the evenings. He'd be sitting, reading the newspaper. Out of the corner of an eye, he'd notice his shadow on the wall scratch the recognizably aquiline gloaming cast by his nose. Then he'd realize, with a start, that, all the time, he'd been holding the paper tightly in both hands, with no itch in his nose at all. Or his shadow above the TV would raise a cup to the penumbra of his lips, when he had no cup in his hand at all.

At first, the shadows just seemed to make the odd movement on their own behalf, and nothing else changed. He decided that this, too, he'd have to get used to. But he'd have his eyes checked again, sometime or another. That would surely fix it. Later, objects themselves seemed to be moved about. While standing at the phone, he'd see his shadow above the writing desk lift up the total eclipse of a pen. The next day, he'd find his pen lying on the desk, though he was quite sure he'd put it in the pen holder the previous evening. Or his shadow above the kitchen table would, quite correctly, mimic his movements while he ate supper; but go on doing so even after he'd finished. At breakfast the next morning, he'd find the jam pot empty. Well, pens can slip out of holders on their own. And he'd often wondered, as a child, whether marmalade isn't so tasty, it must lick itself just a bit, now and again, when no one is watching.

For Paul, the turning point was reached when shadows seemed to cast him. He'd be doing a crossword puzzle, and catch one of his shadows striding along the wall to the kitchen. The next moment, he'd find himself striding into the kitchen too. To fetch something. "What? Well, at least tell me what kind of a what thing!" He had no idea why he was there. Or why he wasn't still sitting down with his crossword. "Where is that crossword, anyway?" He felt his usual measured calm quite run out, like composure at a strip joint. "Fess up. Which of you damned shadows took it? You're all Christly crooks and con-men anyway."

Being cast by shadows was not something he could ever—Holy Whatevers!—be expected to adjust to. It was not right. Absolutely not right. Surely it transgressed all the laws of the universe. And then several more. He obviously needed serious advice, an ally against such devious darkness. He made an appointment with Dr. Jenkins, for the next afternoon. Not just because Jenkins was an M.D.—Paul was confident that there was nothing much wrong with him—but because the doctor had an open-minded interest in all things scientific.

The next evening, with a pot of tea brewing in front of him, Paul steeped his mind in Jenkins' advice. The doctor had, indeed, open-mindedly agreed that strange things can happen. He should definitely be kept informed of any military massing of shadows. But he'd also wondered whether Paul mightn't have had a small neurological incident, which could, temporarily of course, discombobulate both vision and balance, even fine muscle movement and memory. Anyway, nothing, really, to worry about, healthwise. Paul seemed to be going like clockwork.

Paul brewed away moodily over the strokes and forgetfulness bit. Jenkins hadn't taken him seriously enough. Half an hour passed. He looked at his watch. "Hey, my goodness, the tea will be cold by now. Must make a fresh pot. Hate cold tea. No better than brown muskeg with beaver droppings." It was then that his right hand, without him wanting it to, picked up the teapot and poured him a brimming cup. He saw a sharp silhouette on the wall simultaneously, perhaps even a split second before, pour a full umbra of bone china. Not a drop was spilled, though he struggled hard to let go of the pot. At least from the tablecloth's unstained viewpoint, nothing wrong with fine muscle movement there. Then, to his horror, his left hand raised the cup, without him asking it to. He tried to clench his jaws, but his mouth opened in an unwilling gasp. Brackish swamp water poured in, until the cup was empty. Afterwards, the silhouette on the wall reached out, and placed its empty shadow of a cup on the table, right in front of him. Next to his own cup. The shadows had started casting him mercilessly.

In desperation, Paul made a stumbling run for it. As he lurched past the fuse box, he pulled at the lever awkwardly, and cut off the power—and the possibility of shadows. He felt his way to the bedroom, and threw himself lengthwise on the bed, on his back. The drapes were already pulled tightly closed, as he liked them. The silence was complete: no sound of refrigerator or central heating perpetually taxiing and taking off, on their usual all-night journeys. As his breathing slowed, he inhaled silence like a calming and pervasive scent. There were absolutely no shadows in the room. It was as black as tar. He mused, with relief, that, at daybreak, the room would be uniformly grey, still with no shadows.

He tried to turn over, but couldn't move. Apparently, without shadows to cast him, not a muscle. The night would be uneventful, but a long one. The next day, too. He hoped the cleaning lady would find him, when she came in two days' time. To avoid boredom, he began to hum. His glasses, on the bedside table, kept their eyes wide open. Unable to control his voice box, the hum was a monotone, a dark, baritone voice. It gently breathed out shadows from his past, in one long "aaaah." All night. The hum went from being a chestnut-coloured voice to an echo, to the echo of an echo. The humming stopped. The sun rose. It rose again. No shadows his side of the hill. His watch, which needed winding, stopped. Outside, birds took over the business of maintaining an ongoing "aaaah."

Roger Nash was born in Maidenhead, England, in 1942. Surviving the blitz, and being bombed out of his pram, he was raised in Egypt and Singapore. He arrived in Canada in 1965, and has lived mainly in Sudbury since, though with brief detours to Guelph, and to farm in the Tawatinaw valley, northern Alberta. He is Professor Emeritus in the Philosophy Department at Laurentian University.

Roger is a past-President of the League of Canadian Poets, and is currently Poet Laureate of the City of Greater Sudbury. Though known primarily as a poet, Nash has also published numerous short stories. He gained international acclaim for his title story "The Camera and the Cobra," which won the PEN/O.Henry Prize Story Award, and was anthologized by Anchor Books (*PEN/O. Henry Prize Stories 2009*) as one of the twenty best short stories published in North America. *The Camera and the Cobra and other stories* is Roger's first collection of fiction.